Blaze

Dear Reader,

Who doesn't love hot alpha-male rescue heroes? When I wrote about my firefighters for the Blaze line, I set them in the fictional California beach town of Santa Rey. In this book, we're back in Santa Rey, this time with Jacob Madden, one of the city's finest with a badge. He's a bit tough, a bit edgy and more than a bit jaded.

Until he's blindsided by a warm, funny and adorably wacky woman named Bella.

Problem is, Bella's got a bit of a problem. A dead-guy problem. It's complicated.

What isn't complicated is how these two fall in love—hard!—when romance was the last thing they were looking for. Love tends to work that way.

Happy reading!

Jill Shalvis

Jill Shalvis

THE HEAT IS ON

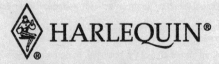

HARLEQUIN®

TORONTO • NEW YORK • LONDON
AMSTERDAM • PARIS • SYDNEY • HAMBURG
STOCKHOLM • ATHENS • TOKYO • MILAN • MADRID
PRAGUE • WARSAW • BUDAPEST • AUCKLAND

Recycling programs
for this product may
not exist in your area.

ISBN-13: 978-0-373-79562-8

THE HEAT IS ON

ABOUT THE AUTHOR

USA TODAY bestselling and award-winning author Jill Shalvis has published more than fifty romance novels, including her firefighter heroes miniseries for Harlequin Blaze. The three-time RITA® Award nominee and three-time National Readers' Choice winner makes her home near Lake Tahoe. Visit her Web site at www.jillshalvis.com for a complete book list and her daily blog.

Books by Jill Shalvis

Don't miss any of our special offers. Write to us at the following address for information on our newest releases.

Harlequin Reader Service
U.S.: 3010 Walden Ave., P.O. Box 1325, Buffalo, NY 14269
Canadian: P.O. Box 609, Fort Erie, Ont. L2A 5X3

To my editor extraordinaire, Brenda.
Thanks for always believing.

1

"OH, YEAH, BABY, THAT'S GOOD," she whispered. So good that she wanted more. She couldn't help herself, she'd never been known for having much self-control.

Not when it came to chocolate. Isabella Manchelli loved desserts, all of them.

Especially hers.

Which was why she was talking to them. Licking the last of it off her spoon, Bella then tossed the spoon into the sink, nodding in satisfaction and pride at the tray of little chocolate Genoese sponge squares she'd created. She wasn't sure of much, but she felt quite positive that the little cakes were her personal best to date. She went to work making up a second batch, knowing her boss, Willow, owner of Edible Bliss Cakes and Pastries, would be clamoring for more for her customers as the day progressed.

And the day had a lot of progressing to do. By the

very nature of her job, she was routinely up before dawn, baking, and today had been no exception. At just the thought, she yawned.

That's what you get for staying up way too late last night...

Having her absolute last one-night stand.

Her last, because as much as she enjoyed the occasional social orgasm, she never got much pleasure out of the morning after. The slipping out of bed, hunting down her clothes from off the floor, carrying her sandals so as not to wake him up...

No, none of that ever felt good as good as the night before.

Even if this time, her first in a damn long time, now that she thought about it, the night before had been so admittedly terrific that she suspected she was still wearing a grin advertising just how terrific...

She angled her stainless-steel mixer so that she could use the appliance as a mirror and turned her head right and then left, inspecting herself.

Yep.

Ridiculous grin still in place.

She couldn't help it. Mr. Tall, Dark and Drop-dead Sexy had really had it going on. She'd met him through the local rec center's singles club, when Willow had somehow talked her into signing up for their Eight Dates in Eight Days. Tall, Dark and Drop-dead Sexy had been her eighth date, and the only one she'd let so much as kiss her.

The kiss had been shockingly...wow. Which had

led to one thing or another, and some more wow, along with a good dash of yowza, and then…the whole morning-after thing.

He'd caught her in mid-tiptoe and off-kilter; she'd decided to go with her standard protocol for such situations.

She'd told him she was moving to Siberia, and then she'd left.

No feelings hurt, no strings. Just the way she liked it.

So why she felt a little hollow, a little discontented, she had no idea.

Probably it was all the chocolate on an empty stomach. Or possibly not. Possibly, the impossible had happened, and her mother's mantra—it's time to settle down, Bella—was right.

And how disconcerting a thought was *that*.

Bella didn't settle well. After growing up one of many in a huge family, she'd taken off soon as she'd been able, loving being alone. Loving the adventure of silence, the lack of planning ahead. It'd been bliss. She still felt that way, still preferred to roam the planet, touching down here and there as it suited her, never staying in one spot too long.

Except this time.

This time she'd landed in Santa Rey, California, the latest stop on the Bella's Train of Travels, and she loved the small beach town. Loved the job she'd taken on as a pastry chef at Edible Bliss, in the heart of a most adorable little downtown, only one block from the beach.

She'd been working here for a month now, and things were good. She had a roof over her head, she had pastries to make, and best yet—she'd gotten that orgasm last night.

Make that multiple orgasms…

She took a moment for a dreamy sigh. It really was a shame that she'd forced herself out of Tall, Dark and Drop-dead Sexy's bed after such a fantastic night, because he'd been both sharp *and* fun, her two top requirements in a man.

He'd also been focused and quietly controlled in a way that suggested cop or military, making her want to break the rules of the Eight Dates in Eight Days contract and ask him what he did for a living. But they'd been forbidden from discussing details like their vocation or age of residence until a second date, if a second date came to be.

He'd been the only one to spark her interest. He'd certainly been the one and only to get her to a bed, and in fact, if things had been different, he might even have had a shot at being that elusive keeper everyone talked about.

With a sigh, she moved through the front room of Edible Bliss, straightening tables and chairs, making sure everything was perfect before she opened them up for business.

She was raising the shades on the windows when she thought she heard a scraping sound from the kitchen's back door. She headed that way, thinking maybe it was Willow a little early. But today was Tuesday, and on Tuesdays Willow took a drawing class at the city college. It was male-model day. *Nude-*male-model day.

Willow's favorite.

It wouldn't be Willow then, no way.

Maybe it was Trevor, the rangy, sun-kissed cutie who worked part-time bussing tables and serving customers.

Walking through the kitchen, Bella peeked out the window in the back door—no one.

So now she was hearing things. Seemed that's what sleep deprivation did to a person. Good to know. Maybe next time she was faced with the prospect of some seriously fantastic sex, she'd say, "No, sorry, I can't, it appears wild monkey sex causes auditory hallucinations in me."

Shaking her head at herself, she checked the Cannoli batch she had in the oven, waving the heat blast from her face. Needing air, she went to crack open the back door, but it caught on something. She pushed, then squeezed through the space onto the back stoop to take a look, and tripped over—

Oh, God.

A body.

It was a guy, in jeans and a T-shirt, a small bouquet of wildflowers clutched in his fist.

Heart stuck in her throat, she dropped to a crouch and put a hand on his shoulder. "Hello?" There was an odd stillness to him she didn't want to face. "Are you okay?" Beneath her fingers, he felt warm, but she couldn't find a pulse. Panic caught her by the throat, choking off her air supply, as did the sight of the blood pooling beneath the man. "Not okay," she murmured, horror gathering in a greasy ball in her gut—which did not mix well with all the chocolate already there.

She closed her eyes on a wave of dizziness, doing her best not to throw up her sponge squares. "Hang on, I'll call 911."

But even as she hit the buttons on her cell phone, even as she stumbled back and stuttered her name and address for the dispatcher, she knew.

The man on her back stoop was beyond needing help.

After being assured by the dispatcher that an ambulance was on its way, Bella practiced the breathing techniques she'd been learning in yoga.

Not helping.

She went to visualization next, trying to imagine herself on the beach, with the calm waves hitting the shore, the light breeze brushing her skin... She had a lot of beaches to choose from, but she went with the beach right across the street because there was just something about Santa Rey's long stretch of white sand, where the salt water *whooshed* sea foam in on the gently sloping shores, and then *whished* it back out again. She swallowed hard, telling herself how much she loved the contemplative coves, the blufftop trails, the dynamic tide pools, all off the beaten path. Here she was both hidden from the world, and yet doing as she loved. Here, unlike anywhere else in her travels, she felt as if she'd come home.

Better.

But then she opened her eyes and yep, there was still the dead guy on the concrete at her feet.

At least he hadn't gone belly up in the kitchen, she told herself, taking big gulps of air. The Occupational Safety and Health Administration probably frowned on dead guys in an industrial kitchen.

Oh, God.

Legs weak, she sank to the ground, feeling weird about being so close, but also like she didn't want to leave him alone. No one should die alone. She set her back to the wall and brought her knees up to her chest to drop her head on them. She was a practical, pragmatic woman, she assured herself. She could survive this, she'd survived worse.

She could hear the sirens now, coming closer. Good. That was good. Then footsteps sounded from the front of the shop, heavy and steady.

The cavalry.

Paramedics first, two of them, tall and sure, dropping to a crouch near the body. One of them reached out and checked the man beside her for a pulse, then shook his head at the other.

Behind the paramedics came a steady parade of other uniforms, filling the small pastry kitchen, making Bella dizzy with it all.

Or dizzier.

She answered questions numbly and eventually someone pushed a cup of water into her hands. One of Willow's pretty teacups.

She answered more questions. No, she hadn't heard any gunshots. No, she hadn't recognized the victim, but then again, she had yet to see his face. No, she hadn't noticed anything out of the ordinary, other than a noise that she'd barely even registered much less investigated....

God.

How could she have not have actually opened the door when she'd heard that odd scraping sound?

After the endless questions, she was finally left alone in the kitchen, by herself in the sea of controlled chaos. She backed to the far wall, attempting to be as unobtrusive as possible. Her legs were still wobbling, so she sank down the wall to sit on the floor, mind wandering.

She wished she'd never gotten out of her bed.

Correction: Tall, Dark and Drop-dead Sexy's bed.

If she'd only broken her own protocol and stayed with him, then she wouldn't be here now. And she might have, if she hadn't been so surprised at how badly she *hadn't* wanted to leave his bed.

That didn't happen often—hell, who was she kidding—sex didn't happen for her often, and certainly not during Eight Dates in Eight Days. She cursed Willow for talking her into doing it, but what was done was done. Besides, it wasn't as if she'd been finding her own dates since she'd put down anchor in Santa Rey.

Date one had been nice but a snooze.

Dates two through seven had been pleasant but nothing to write home about.

But date eight? Holy smokes. Date eight had blown all the other dates not only out of the water, but out of her head, as well.

Jacob.

She knew him only as Jacob, since last names hadn't been given. They'd agreed to meet at a new adventure facility on the outskirts of the county. He'd been there waiting for her, leaning against the building, tall and leanly muscled, with dark wavy hair that curled at his nape and assessing brown eyes that reminded her of warm, melted chocolate when he smiled, which he'd done at first sight of her.

Flattering, since though she was five foot seven and curvy, she knew she was merely average in looks. Average brown hair that was utterly uncontrollable. Average eyes. Average face…

In comparison, Jacob had been anything but average, oozing testosterone and sex appeal in a T-shirt and board shorts that emphasized his fit, hard body. Sin on a stick, that's how he'd looked.

For the next two hours they'd bungee jumped, jungle canopied and Jet Skied, none of which were conducive to talking and opening up, but she hadn't cared.

They'd flirted, they'd laughed, and she'd been in desperate need of both, even knowing he would be nothing but trouble to her heart. She'd had a blast, and afterward, her car had sputtered funny in the lot.

Jacob had said she had a bad spark plug and that he was a car junkie and had extras at his place. If she wanted, he could either follow her home to make sure she got there okay, and then return with the plug to fix her car, or she could follow *him* home and he'd fix it now.

She'd looked at him for a long moment, ultimately deciding that no guy who looked as good in that ridiculous bungee protective gear as he had—and he *had* looked *good*—could be a bad guy.

Naive? Not really. Just damn lonely. Besides, she assured herself, she knew just enough self-defense moves to feel comfortable. She could always knock his nuts into next week if she had to.

And then there was something else. He had that air of undeniable control, that raw male power radiating from him that made her feel safe in his presence. Safe from harm, but not necessarily safe from losing her mind over him. She might not know his last name or what he did for a living, but she knew she wanted him.

So she'd followed him home.

She'd called her own number and left a message. "If anything has happened to me, check with Jacob, sexy hunk, and mystery date number eight."

But nothing had happened to her that she hadn't initiated.

He'd changed her spark plug. And there on his porch, she'd given him what she'd intended as a simple good-night peck.

He'd returned it.

Then they'd both gone still for one beat, their eyes locked in surprise. And the next thing she'd known, she'd been trying to climb up his perfect body.

And she meant *perfect,* from the very tips of his dark, silky hair all the way down to his toes and every single spot in between. Just thinking about it gave her a hot flash.

He'd actually resisted.

The thought made her want to smile now. He'd really tried hard to hold back, murmuring sexily against her mouth that there was no need to rush things, they could go out again sometime.

Sometime.

She'd lived her life doing "sometime," being laid-back and easygoing, not keeping track of anything, much less something that mattered.

For once she hadn't wanted *sometime,* she'd wanted right then. She'd *needed* right then. It'd been so long, she'd been taking care of her own needs for so damn long...

Startling her out of her own thoughts, there was new movement outside the pastry shop as the ME was finally ready to have the body removed. Once again, Bella set her head down on her knees, feeling a wave of emotion for whoever the guy had been, for his family, for whoever would grieve for him.

A pair of men's shoes appeared in front of her, topped by faded Levi's, and she closed her eyes, not up for more unanswerable questions. She heard a rustle and knew the owner of said shoes and jeans had just crouched in front of her.

When she peeked, she saw long legs flexing as he set his elbows on his thighs and waited on her.

He finally spoke. "You okay?"

Wait a minute. She knew that voice. It had coaxed shocking responses from her only last night, and she lifted her head, wondering if her mind was playing tricks on her.

Nope, it was Tall, Dark and Drop-dead Sexy, no longer wearing board shorts and a relaxed, easy grin.

Instead, he wore a light blue button-down that emphasized his lean, hard body, the one that had taken hers to heaven and back.

The man she'd told that she was moving to Siberia.

Oh, God.

He had a detective's badge on his hip, and he was either carrying a gun on his other hip or was very happy to see her, which she sincerely doubted, given the expression on his face.

Gulp.

"Hey," she whispered with a little smile.

He returned the little smile, his eyes warming, but he didn't "hey" back.

Yeah.

She'd had it right last night. She was in trouble with this one.

Deep trouble.

2

DETECTIVE JACOB MADDEN looked into those jade-green eyes and thought *Ah, hell.* What had already been a really rough morning shifted into something else entirely, except he wasn't sure exactly what.

Not only was he running on less than two hours of sleep, he was he looking into the face of the reason for that lack of sleep.

The sexiest reason he'd ever had…

And there hadn't been a wink of sleep involved. Nope, it'd been a physically active sleepover, and just thinking about it had certain parts of his anatomy twitching to life, though those certain parts should be dead after the night they'd had.

Christ.

He knew he shouldn't have answered his damn cell this morning. He hadn't been scheduled to work today. In fact, he'd planned on hanging out with his brother Cord, recently injured on one of Uncle Sam's missions. Today's physical therapy was to have involved the beach, with a net and a volleyball and some good-old-fashioned ass kicking.

But dead bodies always trumped days off, so here he was. It was what he did.

Work.

His job took over much of his life, and it wasn't as if he was petting puppies for a living. Murder and mayhem was his thing, and he was good at it.

But sometimes it got to him.

And in this case, *she* got to him. Bella, with those slay-me eyes, heart-stopping smile and tough-girl attitude, got to him.

"Jacob?" she whispered.

"Yeah." They knew each other's first names, that they both liked adventure and seafood and that they had physical chemistry in shocking spades. He'd held her, he'd touched her. Hell, he'd had his mouth on every inch of her.

He knew he liked her.

A lot.

That had been the biggest surprise, he thought, considering the fact that the guys at the P.D. had signed him up for the date in the first place. As soon as he'd realized he'd been set up, he'd canceled out his singles club profile, but there'd already been one date planned and it'd been too late to cancel on her.

Bella.

He wasn't sorry. Or he hadn't been until she'd walked away sometime before dawn. He'd told himself that had been for the best and, considering her line about moving to Siberia, had figured he'd never see her again.

And yet here she sat, in the middle of his crime scene, looking anxious and stressed. He'd never been able to walk away from a perfect stranger, much less a woman he'd had panting and coming beneath him, so with a sigh, he reached for her hand. "Bella."

Her fingers, icy cold, gripped his. In complete contrast, she kept her voice even. Guts. She had guts.

"I have a little problem, don't I?" she asked.

He found his lips curving slightly. "Little bit, yeah."

Letting out a long breath, she pulled her hair out of its messy ponytail. Wild waves immediately fell in her face. "I tend to do that, you know," she said, trying to corral the hair back into the ponytail holder. "Walk into problems."

Shit, he did not want to know this. "Define 'problems.'"

She blew out another breath.

"Bella." He waited until she leveled him with those eyes. "Dead-people problems?"

"Oh, my God. *No.*" She rubbed her temples. "I really should have stayed in Cabo. That's where I was before this. The kayaking was good, and I was learning how to make the most amazing strawberry-and-honey friand—"

"Bella, about the dead-people problems."

"Right. Sorry. I tend to talk when I find gunshot victims."

"Again," he said carefully. "Does this happen often?"

Her gaze met his. "You're a cop."

"Detective."

She nodded. "I guessed cop or military last night."

She'd made him? "How?"

She sent him a wry smile. "Have you met you? You give off this *I'm relaxed* vibe but really you're totally alert, taking in everything around you."

He took another deep breath and let it out slowly, considering his response. Last night she'd been wearing strawberry lip gloss, her sweet, seductive lips full and curved in an open, easy smile. Her eyes had been warm and welcoming. This morning her lips were bare, and no less kissable for it, but she was breathing a little erratically, and the pulse at the base of her throat was racing.

Dammit.

He'd been a cop since college, a detective the past five years, and he never, ever got used to the punch of empathy when dealing with a victim.

Question was, was she really the victim? "You work here at Edible Bliss."

She nodded, her light brown wavy hair bouncing into her eyes again. Yesterday he'd loved that hair flying free around her when they'd been cuddled up on a Jet Ski, her arms wrapped tight around his middle.

Even later, that gorgeous hair had trailed down his body...

Don't go there, man. "You're the pastry chef," he said.

Another nod. "My lone talent."

He didn't believe that. Last night might have been nothing more than a really great one-night stand, but he'd seen a lot of sides to her. She was adventurous as hell, tough as hell and sexy as hell.

She had layers, lots of them. No way was she just her job the way he was. "You found the victim on the stoop when you got to work," he said, wanting to clarify.

"No. He wasn't there when I first came in." She paused. "Someone shot him."

Yes. Right in the forehead. At close range.

"Shot him dead." Her voice was a little hoarse. "There was blood..." Her eyes went a bit unfocused, and her tan faded to gray. "Huh. I see spots. Black spots. Do you?"

Shit. He pressed her head down between her knees, his hand curled around the nape of her neck. Last night her skin had been warm and silky. Today it was cold and clammy. "Breathe," he commanded softly.

"I'm sorry." She grabbed a shallow breath. "I don't like blood much. You'd think I'd be used to it, given that once I was an assistant to a butcher in Rome, but I'm not. Used to it. God." Reaching out blindly, she grabbed on to the leg of his jeans and held on. "God, Jacob."

"Keep breathing," he murmured, stroking the tender skin of her neck with his thumb. "Slow and deep."

She did her best to comply, sucking in air in a shuddering gulp. "That's it, Bella. Good." Again his thumb swept over her.

"I'm really sorry about the whole Siberia thing," she whispered, eyes squeezed shut, her hands tightly fisted

"Just keep breathing."

"I shouldn't have said Siberia. I don't even like Siberia. I didn't— I just don't do the long-term thing, I'm not good at it, and you seemed— You're a long-term guy, you know? I didn't want to mislead you—"

"Shh. It's okay." Was he a long-term guy? He'd always thought so, but his last two relationships had fallen apart and both his ex-girlfriends had put the blame square in his lap, citing his job, the hours and the danger. So he'd begun to wonder about his long-term potential.

Then he'd gone out with Bella.

He'd been pissed off about the setup, but prepared to make the best of the situation. He'd figured he'd have an okay time, then go home and watch a late game.

Instead, he'd been instantly entranced by Bella's

easy smile, sweet eyes and take-no-prisoners attitude.

He could use more of that, all the way around.

And yet here they were, at a murder scene. He knew she was tough, and he hoped she was tough enough for this.

"There's a freaking dead guy on the back stoop," she said out of the blue. "And I nearly tripped over him. Can you imagine? I actually asked him if he needed anything."

His thumb made another gentle pass over her creamy skin. He couldn't help himself.

Which was why he couldn't be on this case. "Bella, don't. Don't tell me anything more."

"I was here for an hour and a half before I saw him," she whispered, not listening. "Do you think I could have—"

"No." His voice was low but firm. She couldn't have saved him. He believed that much. He looked around them. There were two uniforms and two plainclothes; himself and Ethan Rykes, Jacob's some-time partner. Also Ramon Castillo had just arrived, their detective sergeant.

Shit.

Castillo was a tough son of a bitch who went by the book. Jacob swore to himself and gently pulled Bella to her feet.

"What?" she murmured, still a little gray as she shivered.

Goddammit, she was shocky. He had no idea why

no one had noticed it before, but she needed out of this room and she needed to be checked out. She'd already been questioned, but protocol would entail her going to the station, where she'd be checked for gunpowder residue, and further questioned.

Normally, this would be *his* job. Not today. Not with her. Having been naked with a possible suspect was considered bad form.

There was a walk-in pantry off to the side of the kitchen, and Jacob pulled Bella into it. He shut the door and leaned her back against it, his hands on her arms.

She set her head against the wood and gave him a ghost of a smile. "The last time we were this close to each other," she murmured, "you dropped to your knees and put your mouth on my—"

"Bella." Christ. She drove him crazy. So did the memory.

Because she was right. He had dropped to his knees in front of her, tugged her pretty pink lace thong to her ankles and had his merry way with her.

She'd returned the favor.

"You have to listen to me," he said, looking into her eyes.

"Are you in charge of the case?"

"Yes. *No.*" He shook his head. "I am, but in about two minutes when I talk to my sergeant, I won't be. I can't be."

"Because of last night? Because we—"

He put a finger on her lips. A direct contrast to only a few hours ago, when he'd wanted to hear every pant, every whimper, every cry she made for more. "Yeah. Because of that. I'm not exactly impartial now."

She stared at him a moment, then pushed his finger away. "Am I a suspect, Jacob?"

"As a formality, everyone on the premises will be."

"A formality." She shook her head. "I'm the only one on the premises. Willow lives in the apartment upstairs next to mine but she's in class. The store isn't open." She met his gaze and he was gratified to see hers had cleared.

Yeah. She was tough enough for this.

"I didn't kill him," she said. "I don't even know who he is."

His life had been saved on more than one occasion by nothing more than his wits and instincts. Those instincts were screaming now, telling him that this woman, this smart, funny, walk-on-the-wild-side woman could never pull a trigger to kill someone, much less at close range, in cold blood.

But then again, he'd seen worse.

"Who is he?" she whispered.

"Don't know yet. He had no ID on him, no wallet, no keys, no money, nothing. He didn't appear to drive himself here."

She blinked. "Then how did he get here?"

"I guess we were hoping you could shed some light on that subject."

She said nothing, just stared at him.

At a hard, single knock on the door right behind Bella's head, she jumped, then turned and stared at the door as if it'd grown wings. "They're coming for me."

"No one's coming for you." He pulled open the door and faced Ethan.

"Can anyone join this party?" Ethan asked lightly.

Jacob wasn't fooled. Ethan might look like a big, rough-and-tumble linebacker, with more brawn than brains, but underestimating him was a mistake. Ethan was sharp as a tack, and *always* solved his case. Jacob nudged Bella out of the pantry. "Why don't you get yourself some more water."

When she nodded and moved away, he looked at Ethan.

"What the hell, man?" Ethan asked quietly, his smile still in place for anyone who happened to look over at them. "You screwing with protocol for a pretty face? And don't get me wrong, that is one pretty face…" Ethan turned his head, his gaze slowly sliding down the back of Bella as she walked away, from her wild hair to the sweetest ass Jacob had ever ever sunk his teeth into. "Pretty *everything*," Ethan corrected.

Jacob let out a careful breath. "I can't be on this case."

"You afraid to get tough with Cutie-Pie?" Ethan grinned. "That's okay. Big, bad Ethan will do it for you. I can take one for the team."

"I have a conflict of interest," Jacob said tightly. "And it's your fault."

"Huh?"

"That date you signed me up for last night? It was with her."

"And?"

"And the date didn't end until a few hours ago."

"Nice." Ethan's grin faded as the implications sank in. *"Oh."*

"Yeah."

Before Ethan could say another word, Sergeant Castillo moved in close, leaning over both their shoulders like a bloodhound on the scent. "Ladies, we have a problem?"

"Yes," Jacob said.

Ethan smirked. "Casanova here not only slept with the key witness, but he also slept with our only suspect so far. But at least it's the same person, so…"

Jacob let out a controlled breath and resisted punching Ethan. *Barely.*

Ramon, dark skinned, dark-eyed and tougher than any of them on a good day, quietly stared at Jacob. "Ethan, coffee."

Ethan didn't budge. "I want to hear you chew him a new one."

"Coffee. Now."

"You aren't serious."

"As a heart attack." Ramon never took his eyes off Jacob, waiting until Ethan stalked off. "Talk."

"You remember the guys telling you yesterday that they'd signed me up for a date with the singles club."

Ramon's eyes lit with a quick flash of humor—the equivalent of a belly laugh on anyone else. "Yes."

"It was last night."

Ramon's gaze slid across the kitchen to where Bella was standing in front of a baker's rack, inspecting whatever she had on it. It looked like cream puffs.

They smelled like heaven.

His mouth watered and he wondered if under different circumstances—say, her not running out on him, and him not answering his cell phone—he'd still be at home right this minute, once again sampling her considerable wares—

"Let me take a wild stab at this," Ramon said. "The date those assholes set you up on was with one Isabella Manchelli."

"I guess that's why they pay you the big bucks."

Ramon didn't cut a smile. "You slept with her. Hell, Madden."

Across the room, Ethan approached Bella, fun, laid-back guy gone, cop face on, his pad out.

Ramon let the silence hang between them a minute, then blew out a breath. "Bad timing."

Yeah.

Ramon was quiet another moment, then shoved

his fingers through his dark hair. "Okay, well, we'll deal with it."

They didn't have much of a choice. Jacob glanced over at Bella again. She was still talking to Ethan, but looking past him, right into Jacob's eyes, her own soft and compelling.

She'd planned on never seeing him again, and he'd reconciled himself to that as being for the best.

But fate had intervened now. He wondered just where it would take them, and if they were going to enjoy—or regret—the ride.

3

By THE TIME BELLA finished talking to Ethan at the police station, it was nearly two, which was when her shift ended. She checked in with Willow, who told her that there was still yellow crime scene tape blocking off the shop, so she'd never opened for the day, disappointing their customers.

All those delicious pastries and cakes, going stale...

Ethan drove Bella home from the station. Home was, temporarily at least, one of the two small apartments above Edible Bliss.

"You're new to town," Ethan said lightly, idling at the curb while Bella unhooked her seat belt.

They'd been over this, but she nodded. "Yes."

"You planning on sticking?"

"I don't tend to stick, I never intended to stick."

"Are you...unsticking anytime soon?"

"Not this week."

"Good enough," he said. "Thanks for cooperating this morning."

She'd been raised right enough that she automatically thanked him in return, even though she had no idea what she was thanking him for. Asking intrusive questions? Plying her with bad cop coffee until she was so jittery she was in danger of leaping out of her own skin? He seemed like a good cop and a decent man, but she was on overload now, facing an adrenaline crash. "How long until we can go back inside?"

"Another couple of hours, tops. Just long enough to let CSI finish. You'll call me if you think of anything else you can tell me?"

"Yes," she said, then asked him the question she'd been wondering all day. "Are you Jacob's partner?"

"We work together sometimes, but not on this case."

Something in his voice had her taking a second look at him.

"Conflict of interest," he clarified.

She hesitated, knowing that they both knew *she* was the conflict of interest. "Is he in trouble?"

He started to say something and then stopped.

"Is he?"

"For being with you? No. For not being able to keep his nose out once he's feeling protective about someone he cares about? Not yet, but give him a day or two."

"We're not together. It was…just a one-night thing.

You need to make sure your commander, or whatever he's called, knows that. I don't want Jacob to be in trouble over me."

"I'll be in touch."

She nodded, ignoring the unease in the center of her gut, and got out of the car. She looked at the front door to the shop. Edible Bliss, the cute little paisley sign read. The interior was just as unique. Done up like a sixties coffeehouse, the colors bold and happy.

And just a little psychedelic.

She loved it here.

But at the moment, she also hated it.

There was still yellow crime tape blocking the front door. Willow was sitting on the steps. She was forty, tiny, with a dark cap of spiky hair tipped in purple this week. Her eyebrow piercing glinted in the sun as she watched Bella approach with a worried tilt to her mouth.

It'd been a while since Bella had stayed anyplace long enough to make friends, been a long time since she'd wanted to, but Santa Rey had snagged her by the heartstrings.

So had Willow. They'd spent only a month together, but it felt like more. She sank to the step at Willow's side. "I'm so sorry."

"Not your fault." Willow had sweet, warm eyes and a smile to match, and she hugged Bella tight. "We don't see a lot of murder in Santa Rey," she murmured. "They asked me a bunch of questions and

I didn't get to ask any of my own. Do you suppose they have any leads?"

"At the moment, I might be their only one."

Willow pulled back, clearly shocked. "They suspect *you?*"

"I think it's standard procedure to suspect everyone."

Willow was quiet a moment. "It's probably not appropriate to ask, given what's happened, but I never got to ask you. How did last night go? Date number eight?"

In spite of everything, Bella felt herself soften. "Nice."

Willow blinked, then let out a slow grin. "Honey, a smile that like means a whole helluva lot more than *nice.*"

"Yes, well, it got complicated."

"Uh-huh. Most good stuff is. Is he good looking?"

"Yes."

"Good kisser?"

"Willow—"

"Oh, come on. I haven't had a date in three months. Let me live vicariously through you."

"Yes," Bella breathed on a whisper of a laugh. "He's a good kisser. But—"

"Oh, crap. There's a but?"

"A big one, actually. He's the detective assigned to this case. Or he was, until it was established that he'd slept with the person who found the dead guy."

Willow stared at her. "Oh, shit, Bella."

"Yeah. That about covers it."

They stood together and walked past the yellow tape to the alley between the building and the one next door. It was narrow and lined with two trash cans. Passing through, they came to the rear of the shop, where there was more yellow tape across the back door.

Bella took in the sight of the stoop and shivered. Willow hugged her, then they took the stairs to the second-story landing. Her boss moved to her door. "You going to be okay?"

"Absolutely."

Willow blew her a kiss and vanished inside her place.

Bella entered her own apartment, where she stripped, pulled on her bathing suit and headed back out, walking the block to the beach. The boardwalk stretched out in front of her, but she didn't walk it as she normally did. Today she wanted to swim.

Hard.

This particular beach drew sunbathers looking to soak up the California sun, and fishermen seeking fish and crab. It was a popular spot, and not much of a secret, but this afternoon, there wasn't a crowd. Standing at the water's edge, Bella stared out into the waves, inhaling the warm, salty air. The scent was intoxicating. With a purposeful breath, she let loose some of the tension knotting her shoulders and neck, and kicked off her flip-flops. She dropped her towel to the sand, and then her sunglasses on the towel, and without pause, dived out past the waves. There, she swam parallel to the shore for half a mile, and then back.

By the time she walked out of the water at the same spot she'd started, the sun was slanting lower in the sky, perched like a glorious burning ball hanging over the horizon.

The beach had completely cleared. Instead of the pockets of families dotting the sand, there was only the occasional straggler. She bent for her sunglasses, slid them on, then straightened, coming face-to-face with Detective Jacob Madden.

He looked her over slowly, taking in her dripping wet suit without a word. He wore the same loose jeans and the shirt she'd seen him in earlier, and still had his gun at his hip. The shirt was snug across his shoulders and loose across the abs she had every reason to know were flat and ridged, as she'd spent some time running her tongue across them.

All day her thoughts had drifted to him.

He was easy to think about. He looked great when he was smiling. He looked great when he was just standing there. Hell, he looked great naked and sweaty, and that was hard to do—no pun intended.

He was wearing dark sunglasses and looked like a movie star. She squeezed the water from her hair, quiet as she eyed him. "Definitely Tall, Dark and Drop-dead Sexy."

"Excuse me?"

"Well, maybe *drop-dead* aren't exactly the right words today."

He grimaced, and she had to let out a low laugh. "Are you embarrassed?"

"No. I don't do embarrassed."

But he was. She could tell, and she shook her head. "You do own a mirror, right?"

He ignored that, probably out of self-defense. "I wanted to know if you were okay."

"I was thinking of asking you the same."

"I'm not the one who had a pretty rough morning."

"Are you sure? Because I hear you lost a case just by sleeping with the chick who found the dead guy. I'm really sorry if it was because of me, Jacob."

"I'm a big boy. I'll be fine."

She nodded, but the tension she'd just worked so hard to swim off had come back. Worse, her stomach chose that moment to rumble, *loudly,* reminding her she hadn't eaten all day.

He arched a brow, and she shrugged. "Listen, I've got to go."

"You're hungry."

Usually when she shooed a man away, he went. And stayed gone.

Not Jacob. He stood there, hands on hips, unconcerned that she'd just dismissed him. "I'm thinking they can hear your stomach in China. Let's get something to eat."

Here was the problem. She wanted to gobble *him*

up. But she wasn't going to get him in any more of a bind. "I'm fine." Again her manners got the better of her. "But thank you."

He was quiet a moment, then blew out a breath when she shivered. He bent for the towel she'd left on the sand and handed it out to her. "Bella, I—"

"Look, I hate that you got in trouble for me, okay? And I know you did." She dried herself off.

"I'm not in trouble."

"You got taken off the case!"

"I *took* myself off the case. Officially." He paused. "Unofficially, I'm still involved."

"What does that mean?"

"Let's just say I feel invested."

"In the dead guy?"

He just looked at her.

In her. "Oh, no. *No*." She added a head shake. "You aren't going to risk your job for me."

"I'm not risking anything. I'm off duty at the moment, and my time is now my own, however I wish to spend it. Turns out I wish to spend it helping you."

"You think I need help?"

"I think, if nothing else," he said with terrifying gentleness, reaching for her hand, "that you could probably use a friend."

Dammit. Her throat burned. Too much swimming in the sun. Too much caffeine at cop central. Too much adrenaline still flowing. But it had nothing, nothing at all, to do with having him at her side. "I really didn't kill him," she whispered.

"Well, that makes this a lot easier." Not letting go of her, he tugged her close, looking into her eyes. "How about we figure out who did."

She bowed her head a moment and watched the water drip from her, vanishing into the sand at her feet.

Jacob pulled off her sunglasses and then his, studying her face with his cop's eyes. "You look done in."

"I—" Yeah. Yeah, she was.

Without another word, he tugged her hand again, leading her across the beach to the boardwalk. Willow's shop was off to the right, but he went left.

"Hey," she said.

He didn't answer. He didn't say a word, in fact, until they'd crossed the beach, stepping onto the back deck of Shenanigans, a lovely outdoor café, one of Bella's favorites. Her favorite, because they bought their desserts from Edible Bliss, Bella's own creations, serving them for their nightly dinner run. Jacob pulled out a chair for her and she shifted on her feet. "I'm all wet."

Jacob had slid his dark sunglasses back on, but she felt his gaze go from mild to scorching in zero point four.

Her body answered the call.

"I meant from the ocean," she clarified wryly. "I'm wearing a bikini here, Jacob."

"Trust me, I noticed."

Her belly executed a little flutter. She told herself

it was nerves and an empty stomach, but that was one big fat lie.

It was all Jacob.

He excited her. Even just sitting across from her the way he was, slouched in his chair, long legs spread carelessly out in front of him, just breathing and watching her, he excited her.

"It's a no shirt, no shoes, no service sort of place," she said.

"Fine." He started to shrug out of his button-down.

"Wait— What are you doing?" she asked in a horrified whisper.

"Helping you out with the shirt part." Beneath, he wore a pale blue T-shirt advertising some surf shop in Mazatlán.

And a lot of lean muscles.

A *lot*.

Not that she was noticing.

The light in his eyes said that he noticed her noticing, so she made a conscious effort to shut her mouth and surreptitiously check for drool.

Jacob stood up and walked around to the back of her chair, draping the shirt over her shoulders.

It was warm from his body heat, and it smelled like him, and she had to work at not moaning out loud. Her eyes drifted shut.

Bending so that his mouth brushed her ear, he murmured, "Stand up, Bella."

As if her brain had disconnected from her body, her body obeyed. She stood up.

Still behind her, he guided her hands through the sleeves and rolled the cuffs up, the insides of his arms grazing the sides of her breasts. "Better?"

"Uh-huh," she managed brilliantly. *God, please let me find the bones in my knees so I don't collapse to the floor in a puddle of longing...*

His fingers were sure and firm as he buttoned her up, but somehow gentle, too, evoking memories of last night.

Of course, he'd been *removing* her clothes then, with lots of hot, openmouthed kisses and hands stroking down her body in a way that had brought pleasure and heightened her need and hunger.

As if she'd needed help with the heightening.

Hell, by the time he'd slid his clever, knowing fingers between her thighs, she'd been primed to go off.

And go off she had, like a bottle rocket.

At the memory, her nipples hardened even more. She clasped his shirt to her, her fingers brushing his. "Thanks."

He nodded.

And yet neither of them moved for a long beat. They just stood there, locked in an embrace, her back to his front, his arms around her.

A few customers walked by and broke the moment. Bella slid back into her chair.

Jacob's gaze ran the length of her, a light in his eyes that said arousal, and just a hint of possessiveness.

Clearly, he liked the look of his shirt on her.

Her nipples throbbed. She felt them shrink to two tight points. And thanks to her very wet bathing suit, the shirt immediately suctioned to her breasts so that he could see her happy nipples. "Not good," she muttered, hugging herself.

His mouth curved in a slow smile that heated her up almost as much as the shirt had. "Depends on your point of view."

4

JACOB LOOKED AWAY from Bella when the waitress came to their table. "Hey, handsome," she said. "On duty?"

He'd known Deb since high school. "Not today." He glanced back at Bella, who gave a little wince, making him wonder if she still felt responsible for the fact that he wasn't working.

He didn't want her to feel guilty. In his life, there was *always* work. Hell, there'd be work tomorrow.

Today, he wanted to make sure she was okay. And he could tell by her pallor, by the dull look in her eyes, that she wasn't.

"So what can I get for you kids?" Deb asked.

Bella didn't answer. She was staring down at her menu, already lost in thought, a million miles away. "Bella?"

No answer.

Jacob turned to Deb and ordered for them both.

"Something to drink?" Deb asked.

Again he glanced at Bella. Still looking a little shell-shocked. He'd seen this a hundred times. It'd finally all caught up with her. She was worrying her napkin between her fingers in a motion of anxiety, and he covered her cold hand with his.

She jerked and met his gaze. "I'm sorry, what?"

"A drink? You want some hot tea to warm you up?"

She mustered a smile. "That'd be nice."

Not moving his eyes off hers, he spoke to Deb. "We'll take whatever comes up first, Deb, thanks." And when she'd smiled and moved off, he kept his hand on Bella's.

"You ordered for me?"

"Only because you didn't." His thumb brushed over the backs of her fingers.

"Sorry. What are we having?"

"Pizza, fully loaded. Also a sushi platter and a turkey club."

"For you and what army?" she teased.

Deb came back with the hot tea and some crackers. Jacob opened the crackers while Bella doctored her tea. He handed her a cracker and waited while she ate it. Sure enough, less than a minute later, her color came back, which relieved him. "How long since you've eaten, Bella?"

"Do my sponge cakes and cannoli count?"

"Yeah. Against you."

"Hey, I'll have you know they're the best cannoli on the planet."

He was watching her carefully, noting her fingers shook when she reached for her tea. "Is there someone I can call to stay with you tonight? Family?"

"God, no." She looked at him, seemed to realize that hadn't eased his worry and sent him a little smile. "I have family, Jacob. Don't look so concerned. Six sisters, five brothers-in-law, four grandparents, and at last count, twelve nieces and nephews. They all live in Maine within a three-block radius. If you contacted any of them, they'd roll their eyes and ask what I've done to warrant trouble now, and then converge on Santa Rey like the Second Coming. They'd huddle and hover and nag and smother, all in the name of love. But fair warning, if you call them, I'll have to hurt you."

He found himself smiling. He did that a lot around her. "They're that much fun, huh?"

She shrugged. "We're like a pack of pit bull puppies. Can't stand to be together, but we'd fight to the death for each other."

He supposed that wasn't all that different from him and his brothers. "That's a lot of family—were you all raised together?"

"Yep. Growing up, my sisters and me shared one bedroom with five tiny beds. I was the youngest, so I did without my own bed."

"That must have been tough."

"Nah. They loved me." A brief shadow crossed

her face, as if knowing that hadn't quite made it okay that they hadn't been able to accommodate her.

"I slept with a different sister each night." She shrugged. "You'd think that it might have given me a twisted sense of belonging, but actually, it made me feel like I belonged anywhere."

Or nowhere...

"Which is where the traveling bug came from," he guessed, fascinated by this peek into her life.

"Yeah. I'm definitely uniquely suited to moving around, it's in my blood. I wander, stick for a little while, and if I don't find what I want, that's reason enough to go on."

"What are you looking for?"

She blinked. Clearly, she'd never been asked that question. "You know," she mused, "I have no idea, really. But as I moved from place to place, I learned about baking and pasty making from all different cultures."

"Quite the experience. You must have some great recipes."

"Actually, I don't use recipes all that much. I've memorized the rules and ratios, so I can get away with winging it."

"Rules?"

"Yeah, like egg whites and eggs yolks cook at different temps, and that adding sugar to eggs causes the protein in the eggs to start setting." She lifted a shoulder. "I know a ton of boring stuff like that."

He smiled. "You couldn't be boring if you tried."

The sushi plate arrived, and Bella's stomach growled loud enough for him to smile.

"Shut up," she said good-naturedly, and stuffed a California roll in her mouth, and then a spicy tuna roll. And then another, chewing with a load moan. "God, this is good." She ate for another minute before she seemed to realize he was just watching.

He couldn't help himself.

"You get off on watching women eat?" she asked, looking amused.

"Not usually," he said, having to laugh at himself. "Apparently, it's just you."

A flash of amusement, and then regret, crossed her face, and she put down her next roll. "Listen. I said I was sorry about the Siberia comment, but—"

He nudged her fingers back to her food. "It's okay. It was to be a one-night thing, I get it. But you could have just said so, you know."

"I should have. I'm sorry. But I really have been to Siberia, you know. I used it because it seems like the farthest possible place from here..." She gestured to the beach over her shoulder.

"Why use it at all?"

"Because sometimes guys don't take rejection well."

"I didn't exactly get rejected," he reminded her.

"Because you stalked me on the beach."

He laughed, and she smiled. "Okay," she said.

"Not exactly stalked, and obviously I want to be here or you'd be walking funny."

He arched a brow.

"My signature self-defense move is a knee to the family jewels."

He winced. "I'll keep that in mind."

"No need. Like I said, I want to be here." She paused. "With you." She took a sip of her tea and hummed in pleasure.

"Bella," he said, staring at her mouth. "I love that you love food, and that you seem to experience everything to its fullest. I *really* love that, but you're killing me here with the moaning."

She stared at his mouth in return. "I'd say I'm sorry…"

"But you're not."

Slowly, she shook her head, and when he let out a low groan and had to shift in his chair—she got to him, dammit, like no other—she smiled and broke the spell. "The tea is peach mango," she said. "My sister makes tea like this."

"You ever get homesick?"

"Only for the tea." She paused. "Okay, maybe sometimes for the people. They miss me. A lot."

"They love you."

"Yes, well, I'm very lovable." She smiled again, her gaze holding his. "So, Detective…"

"So."

"You know all about me, and yet all I know about

you is that you feel protective over girls you sleep with, and have a food fetish."

He ignored the protective thing. Fact was fact. "No, I have a watching-*you*-eat fetish. There's a difference."

"Don't distract me," she said, scolding him. "It's your turn."

"To what?"

"To tell me about you."

BELLA SMILED WHEN JACOB just stared at her. The detective was far more comfortable dissecting her than himself.

"What about me?" he finally asked, his eyes shuttering a little bit.

"Well, you could start with why you were one of my blind dates. You don't seem like the blind-date type."

"Is there an easier question?"

"That *is* easy," she said.

He was quiet a moment, studying her. "You might not like my answer."

"Try me."

"Okay, the guys at the P.D. thought it would be funny to sign me up for the singles club."

"You mean, without your knowledge?"

"Yes."

He was right. She found she didn't like the thought of that at all. She picked up another California roll. "So you didn't want to go out with me."

Letting out a long breath, he reached across the small table for her hand, entwining their fingers, his thumb running slowly over her knuckles in a little circle that was unbelievably soothing.

And arousing.

"Bella?"

"Hmm?" She lifted her gaze from their fingers.

"Did I seem all that unwilling to you?"

His gaze was clear, open and honest…and heated.

She remembered the night before, how he'd looked at her as he'd slid in and out of her body in long, slow strokes while murmuring hot, erotic words in her ears, holding her gaze prisoner as he'd taken her over… "No," she whispered, squeezing her thighs together beneath the cover of the table. "You didn't seem unwilling."

"One thing you should know about me. I never do anything I don't want to."

She looked away and cleared her throat. "So, are you the youngest in your family also?"

"The oldest of four boys. I was born and raised here." He lifted a shoulder. "I'd guess you'd say I'm your polar opposite. I like roots."

She didn't correct him, tell him that she was beginning to see the light on that subject. That she'd never disliked the idea of roots, she'd just not felt the slightest urge to cultivate them. Until now anyway.

"My brothers are here in Santa Rey—or least two

of them are. Wyatt's air force, and in Afghanistan, but we think of this as home."

"You're close to them then?"

"Whether we like it or not," he said with a dry smile that spoke of easy affection and an easier love.

It made her feel a little wistful. It also tweaked that odd sense of loneliness that had been plaguing her of late. Sure, she could go home and live near her family, but that wasn't the answer for her.

She hadn't found the answer yet. And wasn't that just the problem. "What about your parents?"

"Retired and living in Palm Springs. I try to see them several times a year."

"That's sweet."

"Sweet?"

He said this as if it was a dirty word, and she smiled. "What's wrong with being called sweet?"

"Not something I'm accused of all that often."

She bet. Hot? Yes. Big and bad? Yes and yes. But the sweetness he had buried pretty deep. Still, it was undeniable. "I have to tell you, I'm sitting here, trying to figure out why your friends thought you needed help enough to set you up with the singles club."

"It was a joke."

"Rooted from what?"

"Christ, you're persistent."

"Uh-huh, it's my middle name. Spill, Detective."

He let out a low, slow breath. "I live the job."

"Lots of people live the job. Hell, I live *and* eat the job."

"Cops are…different. We go to work and tend to see the worst in people every day, and sometimes we face things that make it hard on whoever's waiting for us at home."

"Things like a bullet?"

"Yeah," he said. "Or the business end of a knife, or a hyped-up druggie determined not to go in peacefully, whatever."

"That makes you very brave," she said softly. "Not a bad relationship risk."

"But there are the long, unforgiving hours. People really don't like the hours."

"By people you mean women," she said.

"I've had two serious, long-term relationships, both of whom walked away from me because of the job."

"Were you a cop before you dated them?" she asked.

"Yeah."

"Then that was *their* fault." She squeezed his hand. "Not yours. You shouldn't have to change who you are for a relationship, Jacob." She cocked her head and studied him for a minute, seeing more of the story in his eyes and taking a guess. "So, actually, when it comes down to it, a blind date is right up your alley. Little to no danger of getting too attached, the anonymity of being strangers, et cetera."

"Yeah."

Ironic. Here was the first guy who'd tempted her to stick around in a damn long time, and he wasn't looking for more.

The pizza arrived, steaming hot and smelling as delicious as Jacob.

Almost.

She dug in with a huge bite, and moaned again. "God, this is good." She licked cheese off her fingers. "So why were you waiting for me on the beach? I doubt it was to find out how many siblings I have, or that I have a healthy appetite."

He was watching her suck the cheese off her fingers, but he answered her question without trying to bullshit her, or misdirect. "There's news on the case."

She swallowed and looked at him. "Tell me."

"Have you had any odd phone calls or letters or anything out of the ordinary going on?"

"No. Why?"

"Did you know a Seth Owen?"

The name took her a minute, and she stared at him as shock hit her. "The dead guy. It was Seth?"

"Yes."

"I didn't know his last name," she whispered, covering her mouth. "Seth was date two of eight." Oh, God. He'd been a nice guy, friendly and sweet. He loved puppies and his mom.

And he was dead.

Dead on her back stoop, holding flowers. Her stomach rolled, and she pushed away her plate.

Jacob waited, eyes warm and patient while she struggled with control.

"I keep thinking I could have prevented this," she finally said quietly. "If I'd only looked earlier, maybe called 911 sooner—"

"No. Bella—"

She looked away, toward the ocean, her happy place. The sun was a huge ball of orange fire on the horizon. The late breeze was soft and gentle, but still she shivered.

Because suddenly she was cold, very cold.

"I didn't recognize him this morning," she murmured. "But I never really saw his face, just his back."

And his blood.

"He was so nice. I just didn't— We didn't click." She met his gaze. "I was looking for the click."

She hadn't found that until date number eight, as they both knew.

Jacob's eyes held hers, dark and filled with things, things she didn't intend to spend a lot of time thinking about if she could help it. "I'm sorry. Thanks for dinner, but I have to go." She surged to her feet, needing to bake, needing to be anywhere but here.

He stood up with her, but she shook her head. "I'm okay, really. I just have to…go."

Now.

Yesterday.

He was standing close, looking a little protective

and a whole lot intense, but when he reached for her, she took a step back.

He dropped his hand. "Bella."

"I'm okay," she whispered.

Not arguing with her, he nodded slowly, his see-all eyes taking her in carefully.

"Look, I'm sure you're used to this…murder thing," she said. "But I'm going to need some processing time."

"Understandable."

She ran her hands down herself, realizing she didn't have any pockets. Or money. Hell, she was barely dressed. "I don't have any cash, but I'll—"

"I've got it, Bella."

"See? Sweet." She hugged herself, her fingers brushing over the material of his shirt. "And your shirt. I promise I'll get it back to you—"

"It's okay."

She nodded, grabbing her towel and backing away from him and the table. "Thanks for…" *Everything.* "You know. Coming by, feeding me, et cetera."

"Bella—"

She didn't stick around to hear what he had to say.

Couldn't. She needed to blot out the images of that innocent man bleeding on the shop stoop. She needed some time to untangle the newly complicated knot that now represented Jacob. She needed to breathe, to find some sort of center.

She needed to bake.

5

BELLA WALKED BACK TO Edible Bliss to find Ethan sitting on the steps that led up to the two apartments above the shop. Unable to summon the most basic of manners, she stared at him and sighed. "Didn't I already give you the better part of my day?"

"You had two calls."

"What?"

"Yeah, you left the window open in the shop's kitchen—" He gestured above his head. "So when the phone rang, I could hear the machine pick up. Mrs. Windham wants a three-tiered lemon birthday cake for her pug for next Wednesday, and Trevor wanted to see if you want to go for a sail."

"Is that why you're here, to play assistant?"

"Victim has been identified," he said. "Seth Owen."

Grateful to Jacob for breaking the news first, she nodded and hugged herself. "Date number two."

Ethan pulled a small pad from his pocket and wrote something down. "From Eight Dates in Eight Days."

"Yes."

Ethan made another note. "And you hadn't seen nor heard from him since you went out?"

"I didn't say that." She sighed when Ethan lifted his hand and looked at her. "He called me, asking for another date. I reminded him of the rules, that we weren't supposed to go out with anyone again until all eight dates were over."

"And?"

"And he said he'd call after all eight dates, if I was interested."

Ethan was watching her carefully. "To which you replied…?"

She sighed. "That I'd be moving out of the area."

Ethan arched a brow. "You blew him off."

"I—" She hesitated. Yeah. She had. "He was a perfectly nice guy, I just didn't feel any sparks."

And now he was dead.

"So why was he at Edible Bliss?"

"I don't know."

"Good enough, thanks." Ethan pocketed his pad. "I'll be in touch." He moved past her, and when Bella turned to watch him leave, found Jacob behind her.

The two men exchanged long looks. There was

some sort of silent communication, then Ethan nodded and walked away.

"What was that?" Bella asked. "That whole conversation you just had without words? And you followed me."

"Yep." Ignoring her first question, he brushed past her, grabbing her hand as he did, pulling her up the stairs. At her door, he held out his hand.

"What?"

"Your key."

She stared at him.

"I want to look inside," he said. "And make sure you're safe."

The thought that she might not be hadn't occurred to her. She stared at her door and shivered.

"I'm not trying to scare you," he said quietly. "But you need to be aware of your surroundings. Have an escape route, always. When you walk up these stairs alone at night, you don't have a lot of choices on this small landing."

"I can defend myself."

"How?"

"I'd kick him in the nuts."

He nodded. "Good. But you might need a backup plan. I can show you some moves, if you'd like."

Yes. She'd like to see some of his moves.

Especially if they were anything like the moves he'd shown her last night.

"Key?" he repeated.

She hesitated, knowing he wasn't going to like this.

He took in her expression. "Tell me the door's locked, Bella."

"It's locked." She let out a low breath, then stooped and pulled the key out from beneath the doormat.

He stared at her as she dropped it into his hands. "Are you kidding me?"

She lifted her chin. "I've always felt safe here."

Until now...

"Jesus." Shaking his head, he unlocked her door and handed her back her key. Hands on hips, he silently dared her to put the key back beneath the mat.

She didn't. She almost wanted to, just to see what he'd say.

Or do.

She was pretty sure he could see that particular wheel turning in her head, so she resisted.

He looked at her for another beat, then shook his head again. "Stay here."

She pictured him walking through her tiny seven-hundred-square-foot apartment like something out of a 007 movie, and wasn't surprised that when he came back to the opened doorway, he was tucking his gun into the back of his jeans.

"Any boogeymen?"

"All clear." He stepped aside to let her in, nodding to the two huge duffel bags lined up against the wall in the living room. "Going somewhere?"

"Not quite yet." She nudged one of the bags with her toe. "I don't usually unpack."

He lifted a brow.

She was used to that look. It was the genuine bafflement of someone who'd centered his life around one place, someone who'd made a home for himself. And she'd seen his house. It was big and open and… guy. There was a large, comfy couch and a huge TV. He'd had sports equipment lining his foyer and dishes in his sink. It'd been warm and lived in, and had reflected his personality.

It'd definitely been a home.

She'd not really had a home in years, and never one she'd made for herself since she tended to leave before she wore out her welcome. She realized that she was a contradiction—wanting to belong, yet doubting it would ever happen. But it was who she was. "It's easier," she said. "This place came fully furnished. I'm just borrowing the space."

He absorbed that, looking as if he might say more, but he didn't. And she was glad. She thought maybe they could have a good thing, and she was afraid to hope that this one time, she'd be able to stick around for a while.

He walked past the tiny kitchen table, upon which sat her ratty old notebook.

Last night, she'd written in her journal. It wasn't a typical journal filled with thoughts and expressions, but held notes of her cooking adventures. Desserts were truly her happy place, and she could think about them, or write about them, all day. She'd meant it when she'd told Jacob that she didn't follow recipes, instead using ratio, temps and conversion rates permanently in her brain. Mostly she went with her gut, and with the formulas she knew worked, things like her 1-2-3 method for sweet-crust pastries, which meant one part sugar, two parts butter and three parts flour.

But at the end of the day, if she'd done something new, she liked to scribble it down, and she did mean scribble.

Since she was always in a hurry, her handwriting was pretty much chicken scrawl, and illegible to anyone but her.

"Practicing your Greek?" he asked, raising a brow, proving her point by being unable to read her writing.

"Make fun of my writing all you want," she said, lifting her chin. "Maybe those are *secret* recipes. Maybe I use a special decoder ring. You can never be too careful."

He flipped the notebook closed. Beneath it was a shopping list.

Also nearly illegible.

He grinned. "So you do have a fault. You can't write worth shit. Ever think of taking up medicine?"

"Hey."

He just smiled at her, and it pretty much diffused any righteous indignation she might have mustered.

He came up close and swept a stray strand of

hair back from her face. "You're going to lock up behind me."

She saluted him. Her little attempt at levity. When he didn't smile, she rolled her eyes and nudged him in the chest. His very hard, very warm chest. "I'm a big girl," she said softly, leaving her hand on him. Maybe she even gently ran her hand from one pec to the other. She couldn't help it, he was built. And the way he was standing over her, big and bad and protective, doing his cop thing...

"Bella."

And God, his voice, all low and warning, and completely sexy.

He wanted her again.

And he didn't want to want her again.

Well, welcome to her club. "Thanks for making sure I got home okay," she said. "Did you check my closet for monsters?"

"Your closet's monster free. So's your shower. Nice underwear, by the way."

She'd hand washed a bunch of it and had left it hanging in the shower to dry. She grinned. "Did you like the black lace?"

"Yeah, I liked the lace. And the yellow satin thong and matching bra."

Her nipples got perky. This was becoming a habit. She wondered if there was documentation of Pavlovian response involving sexily voiced innuendo and nipples. There should be.

Then he leaned in and put his mouth to her ear.

"And while I bet they look hot on you, they're not my favorite. At least not on you."

She'd left her hand on his chest, and her fingers involuntarily fisted in his T-shirt.

"W-what is?"

Backing her to the door, he put a hand on either side of her head against the wood and let his knee touch hers. "Nothing at all."

Oh, God.

His thigh slid in between hers, and desire skittered across her belly, heating her from the inside out. "Yeah?"

His mouth skimmed her jaw. "Oh, yeah. But back to keeping yourself safe." He had her pinned to the door, their bodies flush. She couldn't have fit one of her wafer-thin phyllo pastry sheets between them. She squirmed, trying to get even closer, and discovered to her delight that either his gun had moved to his crotch, or he was hard.

"Do you remember what I told you, Bella?" He ran his lips over her jaw and she let out a helpless moan.

"Um—"

He nuzzled just beneath her ear, and she lost her concentration. "Don't keep the key beneath the mat?" she managed to say.

"Before that."

"You told me—" His mouth was on her neck. He drew on a patch of skin and sucked. "Oh, God, Jacob."

"Told you what, Bella?" He dipped his tongue into the hollow at the base of her throat.

"T-to have an escape route." God. God, she needed another taste of him. Just one. "You're it tonight, Jacob. You're my escape." She lifted her mouth and he met her halfway. His hands slid from the wood to her, one cupping the back of her head, the other sliding down her body with a new familiarity that thrilled, and as he devoured her mouth, she couldn't hold back her moan.

He reached for her shirt—*his* shirt—pulling it open, making his hands comfortable on her bare skin, gliding them up her bare thighs, over her back, making her moan again. She felt those fingers catch on the back tie of her bathing-suit top, a light tug, and then it loosened over her breasts. "Jacob?"

"Yeah?"

"My bed's about ten steps away."

His fingers went still. Then he kissed her lips softly and dropped his forehead to hers, breathing heavy. "This can't happen," he said.

She rocked against his raging hard-on. "Hate to break it to you, but your body is in disagreement."

He looked down at his hands. One cupped her breast, his thumb slowly rasping back and forth over her nipple, making it stand up to attention for him, his other was spread wide over her hip, his fingers beneath the material of her bikini bottoms. He still had a hard thigh thrust between hers, and with a muscle ticking in his jaw, he closed his eyes.

Bella's hands had been busy, too. Her fingers were curled in the waistband of his jeans, heading for the hidden treasure. When she wriggled them, he groaned. Grabbing her wrist, he dropped his head to the door, hard.

"What are you doing?"

"Knocking some sense into myself." He opened his eyes and stepped back, face tight, body tense, erection threatening to burst the buttons on his Levi's. "I'm leaving now."

"But—"

His hot gaze swept down her body one more time. He pressed in close, kissed her hard and just a little bit rough, and loving it, she kissed him back in the same way, but then he was pulling free, shaking his head as he moved away. He shoved his hands into his pockets as if he didn't quite trust himself. "We can't— I can't sleep with you while this case is open."

"It's not your case."

He let out a long, slow breath, as if struggling for control. "You need to be careful with what you're saying to me. Only last night, you wanted me to think you were moving to Siberia."

This was unfortunately true. "Yes, but there's something I didn't anticipate."

He just looked at her.

How to explain that last night, when he'd been pulling off her clothes, his hands everywhere on her, both demanding and somehow gentle at the same time, she'd been aware even then that being with him was going to be different.

Better than anything she'd known.

It'd scared her in the heat of the moment. But now, she wanted to experience it again.

Just one more time…

The fact was, in the dark of the night, he'd made her body sing the Hallelujah Chorus, and in the light of day her body wanted a repeat. "We seem to have a little chemistry problem."

He didn't move, but she could see the agreement in his eyes. Plus, he was still hard. Gloriously hard. Her fingers itched to touch, and she reached for him to do just that, until his words stopped her.

"How long are you staying in Santa Rey?"

"I don't know. Why? Trying to figure out if this still qualifies as a one-night stand?" She smiled. "Because I have no problem with a two-night stand. Maybe even a three-night stand if you play your cards right. And by the way, I don't have an aversion to daytime sex, either."

He ran his gaze over her features. Finally, he turned to the door.

"Let me guess," she said to his back, fascinated by the play of muscles as he reached for the handle. "This time it's you who's moving to Siberia?"

When he looked back at her, the heat was still in his gaze. His mouth barely curved in a hint of a smile, testosterone leaking from his every pore. "No. I stick, remember?"

"Then?"

"Maybe I'm just giving you time to absorb what's happened."

"The murder?"

"The fact that we're drawn to each other like a moth to the flame. The fact that it's only a matter of time before I get you in bed again—if you're still around. And this time, there'll be no pretty lies at the end. It is what it is."

Every single erogenous zone in her body quivered. "And what is it?"

He flashed her a wicked, naughty grin, and opened the door. "Lock the door," he said, and then he was gone.

JACOB DROVE HOME TO his ranch-style house in the sprawling, rolling hills that backdropped Santa Rey. He'd bought the house back when it was a piece of shit and no one had wanted to live all the way out here, and as a result, he'd gotten it and the land damn cheap. Good thing, as he could never afford it now that the area was in fashion.

He'd slowly fixed the place up one room at a time, using his own hands and cheap labor—his brothers. He'd found that for the price of beer and pizza, he could coax them out on the weekends, and as a result, his place had become Madden central.

So he wasn't all that surprised when he pulled up and found Cord and Austin in his backyard, drinking his beer and idly watching his two horses roam the pen they'd all worked on putting up.

Austin handed him a beer.

Cord offered an opened tin of cookies, half-empty.

No one spoke until Jacob had taken a long pull from the beer and put away two chocolate-chip cookies, obviously homemade. Since Cord could burn water, he said, "Tell Lexi these were amazing."

Cord grinned stupidly. He'd finally gotten smart and for the last month had been dating his sweet, sexy next-door neighbor, a woman who would most definitely give Cord a run for his money.

"Long day, I hear," Austin said. He was a private investigator working insurance fraud, but his office monitored the police scanners. "You caught a murder."

"And lost it." Jacob took another pull of his beer and told them the story, making sure to face Cord as he spoke, since his brother still suffered fifty percent hearing loss from the explosion he'd lived through overseas.

"So you boinked the prime suspect." Cord shook his head and grinned. "And I thought I was the screwup."

"Bella didn't commit murder," Jacob said.

"So I guess that means you've taken interrogation to a whole new level," Austin said, cracking Cord up. Jacob sent him a don't-make-me-kick-your-ass look, which only made Cord laugh harder.

Whatever. Jacob took the last cookie and Cord stopped laughing.

"That was mine."

Jacob shrugged. "Two types of people in this house. The fast and the hungry."

Cord watched the cookie vanish into Jacob's mouth. "I can go home and talk her into making me more." He added a love-struck little smile, and both Austin and Jacob stared at him. Each of them had had women in their lives before, plenty of them.

None had stuck.

But there was a different element to his brother's expression lately, an inexplicable light in his eyes that signalled something that they hadn't seen in a long time.

Happiness.

After the hell Cord had been through with his long, painful recovery, he deserved that. So very much, he deserved it, and Jacob was happy for him.

And also just a little envious.

THE NEXT MORNING, JACOB found Ethan waiting for him in his office. He'd made himself at home, sitting back in the guest chair, feet up on Jacob's desk, legs crossed as he sipped coffee and thumbed through his iPhone.

"Something new on the case?" Jacob asked him.

"Crime lab lifted a tread print from the top step to Edible Bliss's back door," Ethan said. "They're working on tracing it." He looked up from his phone. "And I thought you were staying out of this one."

"I am."

"Yeah?" Ethan cocked his head. "Is that why you saw Bella last night?"

"We went out for a bite. I walked her home to make sure she got there safely."

"Dude, I came back to ask her a question and heard someone pressing someone up against her front door."

When Jacob narrowed his eyes, Ethan smiled. "I was going to ask her if Seth Owen had brought her flowers on their first date. But I heard that rustling up against the door and figured you two…had your hands full."

Jacob had no response to make because it was true. He'd had his hands full.

"Maybe you were frisking her," Ethan suggested with a smile.

In return, Jacob suggested something with his middle finger.

"Huh. Again with the no comment," Ethan noted. "Maybe she wore out your tongue?"

Jesus. Jacob drew in a breath, and purposely let it out, refusing to let Ethan push his buttons.

"So. You get laid again?"

Jacob shoved Ethan's feet off his desk and sat behind it. "None of the above."

"No frisking, no tongue exhaustion, no getting laid. Got it." Ethan looked at him for a long moment.

"Makes sense since you're so grumpy." He paused. "You're into her."

Jacob booted up his laptop.

Getting no response from Jacob, Ethan pressed, "So into her."

"Not that it's any of your business, but we're just—" He broke off, because he had no idea what they were just.

Seeing right through him, Ethan laughed softly. "Look, I get it. You wanted it to be casual because women end up dumping us for the job. It's a damn fact, man. But if it's more, it's more."

Again, Jacob didn't answer. Didn't know how to answer.

"Fine. Be the big, strong, silent type." Ethan rose lithely to his feet. "But if she's nothing to you, maybe when this is all over, she'll go out with me."

Jacob slid him a long look.

"You know, since you're not into her or anything."

And though Ethan was an ass, he wasn't stupid. He was quickly out the door, a wide, obnoxious grin in place.

Probably if Jacob had consumed any caffeine yet, he'd have caught up with him and pounded him into dust. Probably he could have done it even without the caffeine, except for one thing.

Ethan was right.

Jacob was into Bella.

Luckily, his workload was off the charts, and he

managed to keep busy the entire day. First he was called out as backup on a domestic violence case. They had to pull the wife off her husband, and were listening to the man's side of the story when the wife hit the guy over the head with a flowerpot, right in front of Jacob and his partner. A few minutes later, Jacob was reading the woman her rights, the husband standing there dripping blood, potting soil and daisies.

Boggled the mind.

In the afternoon, he sat in a hot car for two hours staking out a corner near Fourth Street with binoculars, hoping to catch sight of a known identity thief he'd been trying to pull in. By six o'clock, he'd seen a handful of public sex acts, one or two of which had surprised even him, but not a single sign of his man. By the time he got back to his desk, it was far past dinnertime.

But his paperwork had piled up, threatening to topple over. It took him two more hours to make even a dent, and by then, he was starving. He shut down his computer and was nearly to his motorcycle, when a call came in.

Another shooting.

Instead of going home, he met Ethan on scene. "Male, shot once with a through-and-through hit to the thigh," Ethan told him.

"Connected to the first shooting at Bella's place?"

"Don't know. Going to guess yes, since bullet type

matches. The guy was just coming home from being out all day. He had ducked to tie his shoe or he'd have taken the hit to the torso and we'd be calling the coroner about now."

"His lucky day," Jacob said. "ID?"

"Banning Jefferson. Ring a bell?"

"No."

"He lives in the building. His neighbor reported seeing an unidentified male running from the scene."

"Anything else?"

"Perp's around six feet and Caucasian."

Much preferable to five foot seven and female.

"Now, get out of here," Ethan said. "I'm going to nail his ass and I don't want any technicalities holding me up."

"And I'm a technicality?"

"If these shootings are connected, you could be."

Jacob got back on his bike. He needed to go home, eat and sleep.

But first he wanted to make sure Bella was okay. He'd just follow up, he assured himself, and it had nothing to do with their obvious sexual chemistry.

Nothing at all...

Ten minutes later, he was in front of her building. There were no parking spots. With no qualms whatsoever, he parked illegally, telling himself that the salary raise the city hadn't been able to afford to give him for three years running could be paid back in special parking privileges.

He got off his bike, removed his helmet and was at the bottom of her steps, just outside the pastry shop's back door when he heard a scream.

6

The man standing in front of her was faceless. He had a huge bullet hole where his forehead should have been, and he was reaching for her with a hand that held a bouquet of wildflowers. "Bella," he said in a zombie voice. "Bella!"

She screamed and took a step backward, stumbling in shock when she realized that she held a smoking gun.

She'd shot him.

She'd shot his face off.

"Bella!"

She jerked away and fell out of bed. *"Ow."*

Two big, warm hands scooped her up and pulled her into what felt like a wall of muscle.

Even with her eyes closed, she recognized Jacob by his scent and the feel of his arms, and she melted into him, pressing her face to his throat. He brushed the hair away from her damp face, his warm lips settling against her temple. "Bad dream?"

"Zombies." She stayed there in his arms, the sound of her accelerated, panicked breathing and heart pounding in her ears all she could hear as the rest of the world stopped existing.

Moonlight came in through her shutters, slanting the room in glowing stripes. Jacob was on the floor with her, holding her, and there was nowhere else she wanted to be.

He pulled back enough to see into her eyes. "Better?"

Was she? She tried to figure that out. She was damp with terror sweat, wearing only a tiny tank and boy-cut panties. But there was no dead guy without a face, and she wasn't holding a smoking gun. *And* she was in Jacob's lap. "Really bad dream."

"Zombies?"

She let out a shaky breath. "A dead guy. With no face and a hole in his forehead, carrying wildflowers. Chasing me." She shuddered. "And I had the gun."

With a low, wordless murmur, he hugged her closer. Chilled to the bone, she burrowed in. His hands grazed her arms, her back, her bare thighs—

He froze for a single beat as if just realizing only now how undressed she was. Then she shivered again, and a big hand cupped the nape of her neck. "When I heard you scream, I lost about two years of my life during the time it took me to get in here to you."

She tightened her grip. "I didn't put the key under the mat."

"I know. You had it under the flowerpot. We'll talk about *that* later."

She pressed her face into his shoulder. "You smell good."

"Yeah? So do you." He buried his nose in her hair. "Like vanilla and sugar. Good enough to eat."

She squirmed at that image. "I made cookies."

"For the shop?"

"For me." She sighed. "It's a destress thing." She knew she was wrapped around him like Saran Wrap but couldn't make herself let go. He was strong and solid, and she could feel the even, steady beat of his heart. Hers was still racing. "I'm not dressed."

"I noticed that." If her voice was shaking from adrenaline, his was low and husky. His *aroused* voice, which added an entirely new element to her adrenaline rush.

"Not that I'm complaining," she said. "But what brought you here?"

He didn't answer, and it was her turn to pull back a little bit and look into his face. "Uh-oh." She couldn't see him clearly, but she could certainly feel the tension in him, tension she'd missed before because she'd been too busy recouping from the nightmare. "Jacob?"

"I was just leaving work."

"This late?" It was ten-thirty. A long day by any standards, and she was quite certain his hadn't been spent hanging out baking in a kitchen, or sitting and staring at the waves. He'd been out there, catching bad guys, and probably risking life and limb while he was at it.

"It was one of those days," he allowed, in what was undoubtedly an understatement.

"Lots of bad guys?"

"Always." He paused. "And a late call came in."

More tension, she felt it in his thighs beneath her, in the chest she'd set her head on and in the arms he'd banded around her. She climbed out of his lap, stood and flipped on the light by her bed, because she had a feeling she needed to see his face.

From the floor, he blinked, adjusting to the light as his gaze ran over her from head to toe, slowing at all the places in between. "God, Bella."

"I was hot."

His eyes flared, letting her know exactly how hot he thought she was.

"I have to go downstairs in a few minutes and beat up some dough for the morning." The fib popped out of her mouth automatically. But that's how she operated, always giving herself a way out with a man. She called it her safety net.

Except at the moment, for the first time in memory, she didn't want a safety net, and regretted the lie the minute it left her lips.

Jacob remained on the floor. He leaned against her bed, dropping his head back on the mattress and closing his eyes as if afraid to look at her too long.

His dark silky hair was tousled, as if he'd shoved his fingers through it repeatedly. There was a grim set to his mouth, and fine lines of tension fanning out from his eyes.

"You look exhausted," she said softly, and came back to him, curling up at his side, mirroring his pose but setting her head on his chest instead of against the bed.

He wrapped an arm around her and pulled her in. "There was another shooting, Bella. The guy took a hit to the thigh, and should live."

She looked at him, but his head was still back, eyes closed. "Who?"

"Banning Jefferson. You know him?"

She let out a breath. She didn't, not that it made it any less horrifying. "No. The name doesn't ring a bell." She relaxed slightly, grateful this one at least didn't involve her.

His fingers brushed low on her spine, against the bare skin between the hem of her tank and her low-cut panties. "Bullet type matches." Lifting his head, he met her gaze. "In a big city, this wouldn't be enough to connect the shootings, but here in Santa Rey, we don't get shootings every day. Not even every month. So just having two in a matter of days is enough to possibly connect them."

They were close enough to share air, and one thing she already knew about Jacob, he was good up close. Very good. He had a way of looking at her, of touching her, like now, that made her feel both safe and sexy, and that was a lethal combination.

Suddenly she wanted him to use those traits to help her escape, to forget the horror of finding Seth's body even for a few minutes, and it was all she could do to resist setting her hands on his flat stomach, sliding her fingers over those hard muscles as she leaned in and took a bite of him—

"Look at me, Bella."

She was. She was looking at his chest and wondering how long it would take to get him out of that shirt…

"At my face," he said with what might have been amusement.

As if his face was any less dangerous.…

Adding an assist, he cupped her jaw and tilted it up to his, looking her over carefully with that intense, all-seeing gaze that made her want to confess to state secrets, and also take off what little clothing she still wore. She squirmed a little, working her way even closer to him.

"Are you okay?" he asked quietly.

"Working on it. Jacob?"

"Yeah?"

"I'm glad I didn't move to Siberia," she whispered. "And I'm glad *you* didn't move to Siberia." She brushed her lips lightly over his. "I was really scared tonight. I'm glad you're here."

He almost smiled. "You just want me to check for the boogeyman again."

She dipped her head and brushed another kiss on him, this time on his chest. "That would be great."

"Christ, Bella." He ran a hand up her back, wrapped his fingers around her loose, unruly ponytail and gently tugged until she was looking up at him again. "What am I going to do with you?"

Do me was the first thought that came to mind, but he rose and did his cop thing, thoroughly checking out the small apartment, even looking beneath her bed and in her bathtub.

"There's no one here but us," she said when he came back.

"I know."

"Then why did you search the place?"

"So you could go back to sleep."

Which meant he was leaving. Disappointment settled in her belly, which was ridiculous. She'd been the one to formulate the escape plan. "Jacob?"

He lowered himself to a crouch in front of her, running a finger over her temple, tucking a strand of hair behind her ear. "Yeah?"

Reaching up, she cupped her hand around his wrist. "What are we doing?"

"Other than checking for the boogeyman?"

"Yeah. Other than that."

He looked into her eyes. "No idea."

"Casually seeing each other?"

He thought about that a moment, then nodded. "How casually?"

"Asks the woman with one foot already out of Santa Rey."

Fair enough, she supposed. She'd made a big deal out of leaving, and he knew it.

"And I've done the long-term thing," he said. "It doesn't mix well with being a cop."

Right. She knew this, knew all of it, which in no way explained the ball of discontent deep in her belly. She managed a smile. "I know who you are, Jacob. Being a cop is part of you. No woman should ask you to change that."

"Yeah." He grimaced. "It might be more than the cop thing."

"Such as…?"

"I've been told I can be obstinate, single-minded and doggedly aggressive." He said this with a tone of slight admission that it might all be true, and she laughed.

"Well, hell, if you're all that, forget about it," she teased.

"Bella—"

"No, listen to me." She grabbed his arms when he would have straightened. "Those are the very things that make you such a great cop." And, she thought, a great lover. "You're okay, Jacob, just the way you are."

He let out a slow, appreciative breath, then took her hand in his as he rose and walked to the front door. There he stopped and looked down at her, not smiling, but his eyes were warm as he leaned down to kiss her.

"Bye," she whispered.

"Bye," he said against her lips, but instead of opening the door, he threaded his hands into her hair and kissed her again, leisurely this time, allowing his tongue a very thorough farewell.

Her nipples had been hard since he'd first appeared in her bedroom, but the rest of her body joined the fray now, and she rubbed up against him. She'd have crawled into him if she could. "Keep that up," she managed to say, breathless as hell. "And I'm going to fake another nightmare to keep you here."

He stared at her from heavy-lidded eyes, then backed her to the door and kissed her again, kissed her until she was gripping his shirt in two tight fists. His erection pressed into her, nestling against the crux of her sex, and he made a guttural sound deep in his throat. "No faking anything," he said against her mouth.

"Ah, but how would you know?"

"I'd know," he said firmly, and when she let out a low laugh, he paused meaningfully. "I'm sensing a challenge."

"I'm just saying."

"Saying what exactly?" he wanted to know, all male pride and ego, his expression suggesting she'd somehow questioned his manhood or testosterone level.

She tried not to laugh and failed. "Look, faking

is nothing but a polite lie designed to avoid hurting anyone's feelings."

He blinked, looking genuinely confused. "But why lie at all? I mean, if you're going to fake, then why not fake *not* having an orgasm, so that the guy keeps at it?"

"Huh." She laughed again. "Never thought of it that way."

He shook his head, his eyes still heated, his body still taut and tense…everywhere.

Hers tightened in response. She was going to have to accept that whenever she saw him, this crazy heat would be there. But also there was more. What exactly that more was, she couldn't say, but it was a little disturbing given that she'd known him all of a few days.

And even more disturbing, he made her laugh.

God, she was a sucker for that.

She realized he made her both laugh and want, a double whammy, one she wasn't sure she could resist, or why she even wanted to try.

He was just watching her watch him, another thing she liked about him. He was tough and edgy, a cop through and through, and yet he had seemingly endless patience.

But just behind that patience was hot, simmering passion that took her breath away.

He said her name once, softly, then let go of her hair to slide his hands up her back, and down, cupping her bottom, a cheek in each of his big palms, cheeks that were more than half bared by her scrap of panties. A sound of distinct male satisfaction rumbled from his chest, and he squeezed before lifting her to nestle her best part against his best part.

A movement that had them both stopping to gasp in pleasure.

She didn't know about him, but she was instantly back to quivering with need, burning up with it. Her breathing was unsteady, ragged, making her breasts brush his chest with every breath of air she gulped.

He ran his mouth over her jaw to her ear while his fingers explored her body. "If I stand here any longer, Bella, you are not going to make it downstairs to deal with your dough."

"Yeah." She winced. "Remember when you said I always need an escape route? Well, I usually do, when it pertains to men."

"And what, the dough thing was it?"

"Yes. Sorry."

His eyes were two dark pools. "Tell me to go, Bella."

She opened her mouth to do just that and said "stay" instead.

He groaned and once again pressed her into the door, lifting one of her legs to wrap around his hip, opening her up so that when he rocked again, he slid his erection directly against the core of her. The only thing that separated them were his jeans and her very thin, very wet panties.

"Do you want this, Bella?"

In answer, she took the hand he had on her ass and brought it around until he cupped her. Again he groaned low in his throat, and then his mouth found hers, crushing her lips, his tongue delving deep.

Yeah, she wanted this. And even as she thought it, he lifted her up and turned to her bedroom. Suddenly she found herself airborne and then she hit the mattress with a bounce. With a laugh, she started to sit up but found herself pinned by two hundred pounds of solid muscle, and she shivered in anticipation.

"Cold?" he murmured in her ear, his hands sliding beneath her tank, settling on her ribs.

She shook her head and clutched at him. "No."

He held her gaze as his hands slid farther north, covering her breasts, his thumbs slowly rubbing over her nipples.

A shuddery breath escaped her.

He tugged her tank up and off, baring her to his eyes, and then his mouth.

Already half gone, she shivered again, and panted his name.

He groaned in approval, then stood to strip out of his clothes, stopping to pull a condom from his pocket.

She'd thought she had the image of his perfect body etched in her brain, but the reality was even better than the memory. Clueless to how gorgeous he was, he kneeled on the bed at her feet. His hands hooked in the material at her hip, slowly sliding her panties down her legs and off before he parted her legs.

And then his gaze skimmed down at what he'd unwrapped for himself. "God, Bella. Look at you." He kissed a rib, dipped his tongue into her belly button. "I need to taste you, all of you." Urging her open even farther, his thumb made a slow, barely there graze right over her center, and she nearly came off the bed.

"My toes are curling!" she gasped.

"I have the cure for that." And he replaced his thumb with his mouth and proceeded to drive her right out of her ever-loving mind. She came with such force that her entire body was trembling, and still he didn't stop. *"Jacob."*

"Making sure you aren't faking anything," he murmured against her wet flesh.

She laughed, then moaned as his tongue got busy again, ravaging and plundering as he brought her to orgasm once more before finally releasing her.

When she opened her eyes, he had a forearm on either side of her shoulders and was gazing into her face. She had just enough left in the tank to laugh breathlessly. "Show-off."

He smiled, a mixture of wicked intent and fierce affection that didn't just take the last of her breath but also turned her heart over and exposed its tender underside.

What he did next cracked it wide-open.

He entwined their hands beside her head, murmured her name softly, and then, condom somehow miraculously in place, drove into her with one fierce thrust.

"Oh God, Jacob, *God...*"

He filled her so deeply, so completely, she felt as if he was touching her soul, and her hips rocked mindlessly up to meet his. He nudged her face with his jaw, then looked into her eyes as he moved within her, his thrusts deep and steady.

So good, it was so damn good. That was all she could think, and lost in the waves of pleasure crashing over her, her eyes began to drift shut.

"No, don't close them. Look at me."

Somehow she managed to drag them open for him, open and on his, which were letting her in, letting her see what she was doing to him.

Unbelievably, she was on the precipice again, hovering on the very edge. "Please. Jacob, *please.*"

"Mmm." He nipped her jaw, then her lower lip. "I like the begging. More of that."

She laughed breathlessly.

Eyes nearly black with desire, he rubbed his jaw to hers and her laughter faded away. Arching her back, she wound her legs higher around his waist, gripping him as tight as she could.

Now they were hand to hand, chest to chest, breathing as one as their movements sped up, becoming almost frantic, and then, at the very end, she cried out first as she came, hearing and feeling him immediately follow her.

It was the single most sensual, erotic experience of her entire life, and she wondered for the first time how she would ever be able to walk away from this.

7

JACOB WOKE UP, THE sun shining on his face. He was alone in Bella's bed, which was not only a new experience, but also a little humiliating.

He was a cop, for crissakes. As a rule, he slept light, able to wake at the slightest sound or movement.

And yet he'd slept through her leaving, like the living dead.

Of course, he thought, bleary-eyed, as he looked at the clock—7:30 a.m.—he hadn't gotten all that much sleep. Last night, after having his merry way with Bella in bed, they'd moved to the shower where she'd returned the favor.

And then, starving, they'd ended up downstairs in the shop's kitchen, where they'd pulled miniature raspberry turnovers out of the fridge at two in the morning, feeding them to each other.

Licking the raspberry filling off each other...

Jacob rolled out of bed and recovered his clothes

from where they were strewn across the floor. He had a raspberry stain across his chest in a shape that looked suspiciously like a handprint, and he had a flashback to Bella sitting on the counter, him between her legs teasing her, and her fisting her fingers in his shirt so he couldn't get away.

As if he'd wanted to.

Probably no one would be able to tell what the stain was from, he decided, and grabbed his gun and cell phone from the nightstand. He took a stab at his hair with his fingers and helped himself to Bella's toothbrush.

That was all the easy part.

After he'd laced his boots, he made his way down the stairs. He intended to get on his bike and head straight to work, but the back door to the shop was open and the most delicious scents wafted out, making his stomach rumble.

He needed more than raspberry filling.

Bella, her back to him and the door, wearing hip-hugging jeans and a snug red tee, was talking to Willow.

"I can't commit to the Walker anniversary cake, I don't know if I'll be here next month," she said, and for a minute Jacob forgot to breathe.

"Honey," Willow said, sounding as if she was having the same problem. "You're the best pastry chef Santa Rey has ever seen. Please consider staying longer, maybe the whole summer."

"I don't know." She spoke with real regret and

steely determination. "I was up front with you from the beginning."

"I know, but just think about it, okay? You have the place, you have the beach right here, it's gorgeous weather, and you have a hot guy in your bed. What more could you want?"

"How do you know about the hot guy in my bed?"

"Well, because you've been wearing a just-got-some smile all morning. And because he's standing right behind you." Willow winked at Jacob, and grabbing a tray of fresh pastries, made her way out of the kitchen toward the front of the shop.

Bella whirled around to face him, surprise on her face.

"Didn't mean to eavesdrop," he said. "All the amazing smells coming out of here drew me in."

She tugged him out of the doorway. "I'll feed you."

"I have to go to work."

"Food first." She stared up at him for a moment, her mouth slightly curved.

"What?" he asked, having no idea what she could be thinking when she looked at him like that.

"You look…uncivilized," she said.

"Uncivilized?"

"Yeah." She was still staring at him, eyes warm. "You look sleepy and a little bit rumpled, and a whole lot hungry." She eyed the bulge of the gun on his hip. "And armed. It's a good look on you, Jacob."

He pulled her in and put his mouth to her ear. "Keep looking at me like that and I'll show you what I'm hungry for."

She bit her lower lip and slid a gaze to the closed pantry, making him both groan and laugh. "Bella."

"Hey, you put the suggestion in my head." She gave herself a visible shake. "Food. I have fresh croissants that are, if I may say so myself, out of this world." She grabbed one from a tray on the counter and took a bite, moaning softly as sheer bliss crossed her face.

Last night, he'd seen that look directed at him.

Smiling softly, she held out the croissant. Deciding one hunger at a time, he leaned in for a bite, purposely nipping the tip of her finger.

She sucked in her breath, then let it out slowly while the croissant melted in his mouth, making him moan. She'd been right. Best croissant ever.

Willow came back into the kitchen. Her dark hair was spiked around her head today, and she'd put in more piercings than he could count this early. "Bella, honey," she said, taking in Jacob. "He's wearing raspberry."

Bella looked at Jacob's shirt. Dragging her teeth over her lower lip, she appeared to be fighting a smile. "Uh-oh," she said. Grabbing Jacob by the shoulder, she nudged him into the tiny hallway between the kitchen and the dining area, and pushed him against the wall.

"What—" he started, but she cut him off.

With her lips.

He wasn't often surprised or caught off guard, but she kept doing both without effort. Staggered by the kiss, he slid one hand to the small of her back, the other to the back of her head, holding her to him while she kissed them both stupid, stealing conscious thought and detonating brain cells with equal aplomb.

Breaking for air, she murmured, "Morning. And can I just say, casual has never felt so good."

He laughed softly. "No, it sure hasn't."

"Come on." She led him out to the dining area and with a pat on his ass, pointed him toward a bar stool.

A few catcalls rent the air, and shocked, Jacob looked around.

Most of the tables were full with the usual morning crowd seeking their sugar and caffeine rush.

"Ignore them," Bella said loud enough for everyone to hear. "Sit tight and I'll serve you. I had some trouble with the second batch of croissants, but the third batch is just about ready."

The closest table had four women of varying ages starting at around eighty, and they were cackling like a gaggle of hens.

"Saw you come down the stairs," the one with the candy-red lipstick said slyly, gesturing to the café's side window, where there was indeed a view of the building stairs. "From Bella's apartment."

Great. He'd made the walk of shame with an audience.

The woman across from Red Lips arched a penciled-in brow. She had blue hair and her glasses were perched on the very tip of her nose as she looked Jacob over, giving him bad flashbacks to his Catholic-school days when he'd been regularly disciplined. He still twitched whenever he saw a nun.

But this was worse, especially since he would have sworn the two of them were licking their lips over him.

He shuddered inwardly and looked around for Bella. She'd deserted him.

"You have a little something there on your shirt," Blue Hair said, getting up and adjusting her reading glasses, pressing her face so close to his chest her nose brushed him. "Looks like fruit sauce."

Christ. He backed up, bumped hard into the counter behind him and rubbed at the stain, assuring himself they couldn't possibly have any idea what he and Bella had done with that raspberry sauce, which he was pretty sure was illegal in several states.

"Raspberry turnovers were yesterday's special," Blue Hair announced shrewdly, lifting a hand to touch.

He ducked, dodged her, and then whirled around with a yelp when he felt a hand slide down his backside and pinch.

"Nice and firm," Red Lips said wistfully. "They don't make 'em like that in my age group."

He refused to run. But he walked very fast into the kitchen, realizing what he was. "I'm a piece of ass."

"Yes," Bella said, then came up behind him to whisper in his ear, "But you're one fine piece of ass." She offered him a taste of something warm and chocolate and mouthwatering from a wooden spoon. When his mouth was full, she leaned in close and pressed hers to his rough jaw.

He sighed, having to shake his head. What the hell else could he do? "I really have to go."

She lifted a brown bag. "I know. Breakfast to go."

"Thanks." He caught her before she could move away. "You'll call if anything feels off or weird."

Her eyes laughed at him. "I'm pretty sure I've got the croissants under control now."

"Not that, smart-ass." He tugged on her hair. "If you see anything odd, or someone so much as looks at you cross-eyed, you'll call." Unable to resist, he kissed her. He'd meant for it to be a light, easy kiss, but as usual, he'd underestimated her innate ability to drive him crazy.

He wasn't sure how long he'd been kissing her when he came up for air.

Her eyes were closed and she was wearing a dreamy smile. "Um," she said, and opened those gorgeous eyes, staring at his mouth as if she wanted another.

"You'll call," he repeated.

"Mmm, hmm."

He ran his thumb over her lush lower lip. "I'm going to assume that was 'Yes, Jacob, I'll call if anything seems off, or anyone so much as crosses their eyes at me.'"

With a smile, she pulled him down and kissed him again.

It was a diversion, but he couldn't summon irritation when it was such an effective one. She'd been right about one thing—casual had never felt so good. It took a shocking degree of control to remind himself that he'd only meant to make sure she was okay, that it was time to go, and even then he took a minute to press his face against her hair before walking out the door.

While he still could.

"YOU EVER GOING TO TELL me about that kiss?" Willow asked Bella later that afternoon as they were cleaning up the shop after a day of brisk business.

"What kiss?"

"The one you laid on Tall, Dark and Drop-dead Sexy earlier, the one that looked like something right out of a movie." She fanned air in front of her face. "Goodness, it was hot. That man is hot. The way he cupped your jaw and looked at you for a beat before molding you to every single inch of him…" She slid Bella a long look. "And I have a feeling there are a lot of inches to him—"

"Willow!"

She grinned, unrepentant. "Sorry. I'll stop. It's giving me a hot flash anyway. But just tell me this much—you going to keep him?"

If I can, Bella almost said, but squelched it. Casual. They were going for casual. She'd agreed. And casual didn't worry about things like keeping someone. "Undetermined at this time," she finally said.

"Seriously? Because if someone was kissing me like that, I'd keep him. I'd keep him naked and handcuffed to my bed."

Bella shook her head just as Trevor came in from the front room, carrying a heavy tray of dirty dishes. He looked like the typical California surfer boy with his deep tan and easy good looks. "Getting kinky again, Willow?" he asked with a wink.

"Not me. Bella."

Bella rolled her eyes and headed to the door. "I'm out. I'm going for a swim."

"Hold up." Trevor flashed a smile her way. "You shouldn't swim out there alone," he said. "I'm off, too, I'll come with."

It wasn't a hardship to have his company. He was a strong swimmer, plus he was just damn fine scenery, all tanned and buff and gorgeous. His quick grin didn't hurt, either. But though she'd given some thought to him when she'd first come to Santa Rey, he was younger than her, and they worked together… and she'd decided against it. But no one could blame her for enjoying the view.

Still, she found herself yearning for the view

of another man, a big, bad, sexy detective named Jacob...

After the swim, she and Trevor sat on the sand. "Dinner?" he asked, tilting his head back to the warm sun.

She hesitated. Swimming as friends was one thing. But having dinner, too, might put it into another category. "Trev—"

"Just dinner, Bella." He smiled. "Unless you plan on breaking my heart over sushi."

"I'm taking a break from breaking hearts."

"Didn't look that way this morning."

She grimaced. "Don't ask me what I think I'm doing."

He shrugged. "Hey, sometimes the heart wants what it wants."

She sighed. "Yeah." And sometimes the heart wanted what it couldn't have...

After they dried off, Trevor left to meet up with friends for that sushi he wanted, and Bella went back to her apartment to change out of her wet suit before going back down to the shop. She pulled on a halter sundress in deference to the heat and headed into the downstairs kitchen to make the dough for tomorrow's shortbread, wanting to give it time to rise. She'd just finished when she heard a knock on the front door. Moving through the tables, she saw a face pressed up against the window.

Tyler Scott, date number three. She knew his last name because he was a bookseller here in town. She'd been fascinated by his brains and sheer volume of knowledge, and just a little bit intimidated.

But he was a good guy, a very nice guy, and so she opened the door with a smile. "Tyler, hi. I'm so sorry, but we're closed."

"I know. I was just hoping…" He paused. "I know this is so rude of me to ask, but I'm heading to my mother's in San Luis Obispo and I'm expected to bring the dessert. I guess I was wondering if you wouldn't mind setting me up with something, but now I realize what an imposition it would be, and—"

"No. No imposition," she said. "Let's go see what we have left over in the back."

Five minutes later, she'd sold him a small chocolate sandwich cake, and she walked him back through the shop to the front door.

"My mom's going to take one bite of this and start harassing me to bring you home," he teased.

Bella smiled. There was no doubt she enjoyed his company, but there was something pretty vital missing—the zing.

She'd never really pondered the mystery of the elusive zing until Jacob. Because, holy shit, she and Jacob had zing. They had real, gut-tightening, goose-bump-inducing, brain-cell-destroying zing, and they had it in spades. She hated to compare men, but she could honestly say that not a single one of the other seven guys she'd dated during the Eight Dates in Eight Days had come even close.

And while she was being so honest, she might as

well admit that no man in recent history had come close.

Maybe no man ever.

And wasn't that a terrifying thought all on its own?

"Thanks again, Bella," Tyler said, and stepped outside the door. She followed, wanting to see if the early evening had cooled down any.

A loud shot sounded, echoing in the still air, and the glass window just behind them shattered. Before Bella could even begin to process any of it, Tyler grabbed her and knocked her to the ground.

It seemed like forever, but it was probably only seconds before the glass finished raining down over them. Finally, Tyler lifted his head. "Bella?" When he sat up, his glasses were crooked on his nose. "You okay?"

Her knees and palms were skinned, but that was nothing compared to being dead. "Yes. What the hell was that?"

"Something exploded your window."

"Something?"

"I think someone shot at us." Tyler stood, then pulled her to her feet, as well, running his gaze down her, then down himself. "No injuries. No injuries is good. It means we can freak out now."

Bella stared up at the blown-out window of the shop. "A gunshot?" Oh, God. Not again. "Are you sure?"

There were a few people gathering on the sidewalk,

murmuring amongst themselves. "I phoned 911," one of them called out. It was Cindy, who worked at the art gallery across the street and bought a croissant from Bella every morning without fail. She was still holding her cell phone. "I don't think I've ever heard a real gunshot before."

Bella was still staring at the hollow window, a matching hollowness sinking in her gut.

Looking shell-shocked, Tyler sank to the curb. Just as shell-shocked, she sat next to him. "Can I borrow your phone?" she asked, and when he handed it over, she punched in Jacob's cell number. It went straight to voice mail. "Hi," she said. "Nobody looked at me cross-eyed, but I did get shot at. That probably counts as something you'd like to know, right?" She drew in air. "I'm okay," she said, and disconnected.

He would come. And that brought a now-familiar tingling that yesterday had started and ended in all her erogenous zones, but today...today nicked at a certain vital organ that clenched hard at the mere thought of him.

She remembered how he'd looked this morning sprawled on his back across her bed, the sheets and blankets on the floor, revealing him in full glory.

And then there'd been how he'd looked coming into the shop all rumpled and sleep deprived, a two-day-old shadow darkening his strong jaw, his eyes narrowed and probably already filled with thoughts of his cases, his shirt wrinkled, that raspberry stain over one pec.

Armed and dangerous.

And badass gorgeous.

She might have dwelled on that, but there was the whole just-been-shot-at thing, and the police arrived.

Then she heard the motorcycle. Jacob came off it at a dead run, slowing only when he saw her standing in the midst of the organized mayhem, clearly fine.

Or as fine as she could be.

Normally in a stressful situation—and she considered this pretty damn stressful—she'd already be out the door. Gone. Moved on. After all, she'd grown up in chaos, and it'd never suited.

But she didn't have the urge to run right now. It was the place, she thought. Santa Rey seemed to be making a home for itself in her heart. And so were its people.

One in particular.

Jacob came toe to toe with her. He removed his sunglasses and ran his gaze over her carefully, thoroughly, noting the scrapes on her hands and knees.

"We're okay," she said. "Tyler pushed me down. Thank you for that, by the way," she told him.

Jacob flicked a glance in Tyler's direction and nodded, then surveyed the damage around them with one sweep of his focused, sharp eyes before returning his attention to her. He pulled her to her feet, picked a piece of glass from her hair and shook his head, then slipped an arm around her, tugging her close enough to press his mouth to her jaw. "Calls like the one I just got suck."

"I'm sorry."

He murmured something too soft to catch and wrapped both arms around her, holding tightly now, as if he needed it as much as she. Snuggling in, she absorbed his warmth and strength. After a long moment, she said, "I'm really okay. You can let me go now."

"I'll let you go when I'm good and ready." But he sighed and pulled back, cupping the nape of her neck to look into her eyes. Whatever he saw must have reassured him because he nodded. "You good to talk to Ethan?"

"Yes."

"Good. Because he's right behind you, giving me the evil eye, waiting for me to let go of you so he can ask you some questions. Also, just so you can brace yourself, we're going to put a man on the shop."

"A man?"

"A squad car. We're talking murder, and now attempted murder."

"This is getting old."

Jacob looked deep into her eyes, his own dark and troubled. "There's always Siberia."

"You want me to leave?"

"I want you safe."

So did she. But she'd never felt as safe anywhere as she did right there, in his arms.

8

TWO HOURS LATER IT was finally just Bella again.

Well, just Bella and the policeman assigned to watch over the building. She couldn't see him, but she knew he was around somewhere, and that was just fine with her.

Feeling as calm as she possibly could, she stood in the shop kitchen and let out a deep breath, nearly screaming when she turned in a circle and came face-to-face with Jacob.

Yeah, apparently her nerves were shot.

He'd watched as the EMTs had bandaged up her knees, then helped board up the front window before leaving for a task-force meeting with Ethan, but apparently he was back, looking his usual big and bad and edgy.

She did the first thing that came to mind. She walked right into his arms.

They closed around her, warm and taut with

muscle, tightening on her, surrounding her with his virility, the scent of him. The police had questioned her, Tyler and then Willow, who'd shown up when she'd heard. Trevor, too. The shooting might have been random and unconnected to the other shootings, but until the ballistics came through, no one would know for sure.

Tyler had left, completely unnerved. Probably he wouldn't be a returning customer, Bella thought with a sigh.

"You okay?" Jacob asked.

She'd had to ask herself that several times now, and she wasn't used to not being sure. She was always okay, it was her M.O. And if she wasn't, well, then, there was always someplace new. "Aren't you getting tired of having to ask me that?"

Silent, he stroked a big hand up and down her back.

"For two people who aren't involved," she murmured, "we sure are seeing a lot of each other."

She felt him smile against her hair, and pulled back to look into his eyes. "I've always felt so safe here," she said. "It's why I stayed. I never thought of it before, but I *like* feeling safe. But now someone's shooting at me. I know we joke about Siberia, but holy shit, am I really going to have to go?"

"Would you?"

When she thought about leaving, she felt a clutch in her gut. "No."

He nodded, clearly already guessing as much. "We're going to figure it out."

"We? You mean, the police?"

He made a vague response deep in his throat and pulled her out of the kitchen's back door, carefully locking up.

Then he led her upstairs toward her apartment.

"I appreciate the sentiment," she said to his broad back. "But fair warning, it's going to take an act of Congress and possibly hypnosis to get me in the right frame of mind for sex."

He glanced back at her, his mouth slightly curved. "I'll keep that in mind, but that's not what we're doing. I want you to pack an overnight bag."

"Excuse me?"

His hand tightened on hers when she tried to pull free. "You're not staying here tonight, Bella. Maybe not tomorrow night, either. Not until we know what the hell is going on and why you nearly took a hit today."

"Jacob—"

"This is nonnegotiable, Bella. We have a man here but for tonight at least, you're gone."

She looked into his eyes, fierce and protective and utterly stubborn.

"I'm not saying you have to stay with me," he said, bringing their joined hands to his mouth so that when he spoke, his lips brushed against her fingers. "I'm not trying to exert power or authority over you, just common sense. You can stay in a hotel, you can stay with a friend or you can stay with me. I don't care, but you're not staying here alone. Please," he said very softly when she opened her mouth.

She had a feeling he wasn't a man to say please very often. Touched, she nodded her head, and turned to go into her place.

He stopped her and moved inside first, once again thoroughly checking it out, giving her the go-ahead when he deemed it safe.

Normally she liked watching him do his cop thing. It was macho and alpha and on any other day it would have made her knees weak and other parts quiver.

But not now. Now she wanted the nightmare to go far, far away.

He was helping with that just by being here for her instead of running off soon as he was done being questioned, like Tyler. Willow and Trevor had both left rather quickly, too, soon as they were able.

Not Jacob.

He wanted her safe. He was willing to do whatever it took to keep her that way.

She racked her brain to try to remember the last time someone outside of her family had truly cared and worried about her, and she couldn't come up with anything. This was easy enough to explain. Until recently, she hadn't stuck around long enough for such ties.

She would have to decide if she liked it.

She filled a small backpack, and then realizing

Jacob probably had his motorcycle, she slid on a pair of denim shorts beneath her halter sundress.

They left her apartment, locked up, and in the lot, Jacob nodded to a guy walking the alley between the shop and the building next door.

He nodded back.

"My bodyguard?" she asked.

Jacob actually smiled. "Tonight, I'm your bodyguard." And he handed her a helmet.

"What about Willow?"

"Didn't she tell you? She went to her mom's."

No, she hadn't mentioned that…

"Where are we going?" she asked, getting on his bike behind him, hiking her dress up until it looked like a loose summer top over her shorts. She slipped her arms around him, her hands sliding across his washboard abs.

"For food. You smell like sugar and vanilla and you're making me hungry."

"I have—"

"Your desserts are heaven, Bella, but I need real sustenance. And so do you. You're pale."

And that was new, too. He was a guy who said what he meant, no sneaky charm to try to get her into bed, no pretty lies just to make her feel better. He told her what was on his mind and expected her to be mature enough to deal with it.

Her first grown-up relationship, she realized, "casual" as it was—

She broke off the thought with a startled squeak

when he revved the bike and hit the throttle. The engine roared between her legs and suddenly, blessedly, just like that, her mind was off murder and bullets and she couldn't decide which was better, hugging up to Jacob's hard body, or the way he maneuvered them through the streets as if he were a part of the bike.

She was still trying to decide when he pulled up to a small diner, where they were greeted by yet another smiley-faced waitress ready to serve his every need.

After they'd ordered, Bella looked at him. "Must be tough, being so hated everywhere you go. Have you dated them all?" *Slept with them all…?*

He looked at her for a long moment. "Who?"

She rolled her eyes. "The women who fall all over themselves to make you smile."

"People in Santa Rey like cops."

And he was all cop. He was also all man.

He pulled out a pad and pencil from his pocket and looked at her. "I want to hear about your eight dates," he said, clearly done discussing women, his or otherwise.

"Nice subject change."

He looked at her, torn between amusement and irritation. "Do you want to discuss the waitress— who, by the way, used to babysit me—or whoever's screwing with your life?"

Well, damn, when he put it that way… "I've al-

FREE Merchandise is 'in the Cards' for you!

Dear Reader,

We're giving away FREE MERCHANDISE!

Seriously, we'd like to reward you for reading this novel by giving you **FREE MERCHANDISE** worth over **$20**. And no purchase is necessary!

You see the Jack of Hearts sticker above? Paste that sticker in the box on the Free Merchandise Voucher inside. Return the Voucher promptly...and we'll send you valuable Free Merchandise!

Thanks again for reading one of our novels—and enjoy your Free Merchandise with our compliments!

Pam Powers

Pam Powers

P.S. Look inside to see what Free Merchandise is **"in the cards"** for you!

(H-B-08/10)

We'd like to send you two free books to introduce you to the Harlequin® Blaze® series. These books are worth over $10, but they are yours to keep absolutely FREE! We'll even send you 2 wonderful surprise gifts. You can't lose!

REMEMBER: Your Free Merchandise, consisting of **2 Free Books** and **2 Free Gifts**, is worth over $20.00! No purchase is necessary, so please send for your Free Merchandise today.

YOUR FREE MERCHANDISE INCLUDES...

2 FREE Harlequin® Blaze® Books
AND 2 FREE Mystery Gifts

FREE MERCHANDISE VOUCHER

2 FREE BOOKS and **2 FREE GIFTS**

Please send my Free Merchandise, consisting of
2 Free Books and **2 Free Mystery Gifts**.
I understand that I am under no obligation to buy
anything, as explained on the back of this card.

*About how many NEW paperback fiction books
have you purchased in the past 3 months?*

❑ 0-2	❑ 3-6	❑ 7 or more
E7Q6	E7RJ	E7RU

151/351 HDL

Please Print

FIRST NAME

LAST NAME

ADDRESS

APT.#   CITY

STATE/PROV.   ZIP/POSTAL CODE

Offer limited to one per household and not valid to current subscribers of Harlequin® Blaze® books.
Your Privacy—Harlequin Books is committed to protecting your privacy. Our Privacy Policy is available online at
www.ReaderService.com or upon request from the Reader Service. From time to time we make our lists of
customers available to reputable third parties who may have a product or service of interest to you. If you would
prefer for us not to share your name and address, please check here ❑. **Help us get it right**—We strive for
accurate, respectful and relevant communications. To clarify or modify your communication preferences, visit us at
www.ReaderService.com/consumerschoice.

NO PURCHASE NECESSARY!

▶ Detach card and mail today. No stamp needed. ▶

© 2010 HARLEQUIN ENTERPRISES LIMITED ® and ™ are trademarks owned
and used by the trademark owner and/or its licensee. Printed in the U.S.A.

(H-B-08/10)

ready gone over all of this with Ethan. Twenty-five million times."

"So let's do it twenty-five million and one. Maybe we've all missed something. Names and impressions."

"You think one of my dates is a crazy stalker." She shivered at the thought. "Which doesn't explain the second guy who got shot, the one across town."

"True, but there are a lot of possibilities here. Let's work at narrowing them down."

He was all focused and fiercely intense, and when he was really concentrating—like now—he got that deep furrow in his brow.

She wanted to forget the hell that was her current life and kiss that furrow away. What could she say. Yes, her sexual thoughts were inappropriate considering the moment, but it was a defense mechanism. And an easy one to cling to. For God's sake, just look at him. Still watching him, she reached for her soda and sucked her straw.

Immediately his eyes homed in on her mouth. Huh. Maybe she'd been wrong about needing an act of Congress to want sex. She smiled.

And he raised a brow.

She sucked some more soda down. "About that hypnosis I mentioned, to get in the right mind for sex…"

His eyes dilated. "Distracting me isn't going to end this conversation," he said, voice husky.

"You sure?"

His gaze never left her mouth. "Positive. I can't be distracted. It's one of my gifts."

She was in a position to know that he had other gifts… Lightly, she ran her fingers down the straw, then sucked some more.

Jacob let out a shaky breath. "Okay, new plan."

"Which is?"

"You talk fast, and then we're going back to my place."

"To…watch a movie?"

"Guess again."

A little frisson of heat raced up her spine, something she'd have thought impossible tonight. "Play a game?"

He smiled, and it was filled with so much fire, she nearly had an orgasm on the spot. "Sure, we can play a game. How about Seven Minutes in Heaven."

"I might need more than seven minutes."

"You can have as many minutes as you want." He pulled the soda away from her, and the straw popped out of her mouth with an audible sound that made his eyes darken even more. "But this first."

"Damn. You're so strict."

"You know," he said, "I was hoping I could get you out of that quiet, protective shell you had going, but I didn't think it would happen at my expense."

She sipped more of her soda.

Now he out and out grinned, looking so freaking sexy she could hardly stand it. She had no idea what was wrong with her. She didn't go back for seconds, much less thirds, and yet she had a feeling she could have this man every night until she left for her next destination, and it still wouldn't be enough.

Jacob gently tapped her forehead with the end of his pencil. "Anyone home?"

"Sorry."

"The dates," he said.

Right. "Number one was Bo. Cute, nice, sweet. And too young for me."

"How young?"

"Like five years."

"Huh."

"Huh what?" she asked.

He lifted a broad shoulder. "I doubt he feels too young for you. Next?"

"Seth was number two." She let out a low, pained breath and fell quiet for a minute, remembering him with an ache in her chest. "Date three was Tyler, the bookseller. You saw him today."

"Yeah. What did you think of him?"

"Sweet. Nice. And so smart as to be a little intimidating."

He was making notes. "A dweeb."

"That's not nice."

"Good. Remember that when you're describing date eight, cuz I don't want to hear I'm sweet or nice. Date four."

She shook her head. "A guy named Brady. He seemed..." She nearly said nice but bit it back. "Harmless."

Jacob lifted his head. "Brady, the guy who owns the coffee shop on Third?"

"I think so, yes."

"You think Brady is harmless."

"I do."

He shook his head and kept writing.

Cocking her head to the side, she tried to read what he was writing. "What's wrong with him?"

"What's wrong with him? He dates a different woman every night of the week. He drives a scooter, which for some reason, women think is...*nice*. And he looks like a poet."

"He *is* a poet."

Jacob did a palms up, like *see?*

She held back a grin. "I liked him."

"Did you sleep with him?"

"Is that for your notes?"

Frowning, he wrote something on his pad, pressing hard enough on the paper that his knuckles turned positively white. "Date five."

Okay, so they were moving on. Worked for her. Their food arrived and she dug in. "Juan Martine," she said around her BLT. "I know his last name because I recognized him."

Again he lifted his head and looked at her, that furrow firmly in place. "The model."

"Do you know everyone in town?" She shook her head. "Never mind. Why don't you tell me what's wrong with him, too."

"He wears hair product."

She burst out laughing.

Jacob's furrow deepened. "He does."

"Are you going to find something wrong with each of them? Because it's cute. And yeah, that's going in your description."

This did not help his mood. "I am *not* cute."

She grinned. "You think the word insults your manhood."

"Jesus." He tossed down his pencil and scrubbed his hands over his face. "Forget it."

"Fine. Forget that I think you're cute. I'll never say cute again. Let's go with…" She paused, considering him carefully. "Edgy, grumpy and…"

"We're supposed to be talking about *you*. About your dates. Not me."

"Sexy."

He stared at her. "You drive me crazy."

"Ditto. Can we get back to the rest of the dates, or are you too jealous?"

"I'm not jealous."

"Whatever."

"I am not jealous, Bella."

"Date six. B.J. Sorry, I don't have a full name, but he works in sales, and is a really nice guy."

"What is it with you and nice?"

She ignored that. "Date seven was Lorenzo Ramos, and though I shouldn't know his last name, I do because he's a chef, and works at the Hilltop Lodge."

Jacob wrote the name down and remained silent.

"What, no comment on Lorenzo?"

"No."

"Oh, come on," she said with a laugh. "You know you want to."

"Hey, it's none of my business if you want to date a guy who drives a twenty-year-old Rabbit."

"It saves gas, a lot of gas. And what is it with you and a guy's ride?"

He didn't answer.

"I think this brings us up to date number eight," she said.

"Yeah. Him I've met." By this time they were done eating. He stood and dropped some cash on the table.

"What, you don't want my impression?"

He flashed her an unreadable look, then grabbing her hand, pulled her up and toward the door in one smooth movement.

"What are we doing now?"

"Going home to discuss your impressions of date number eight. In detail…"

9

JACOB'S CELL BUZZED as he led Bella into his house. It was Ethan. "Make yourself at home," he said to Bella. "I have to take this." He moved to the laundry room off the kitchen and flipped open his phone. "Madden."

"She with you?"

"Yes."

"I'm glad she's safe."

There was something in Ethan's voice that tipped him off. "What do you have?"

"The print from the first shooting. The crime lab found marina sand in the tread."

"We need to have the marina checked out."

"Already there. Checking the hotels, motels and all the boats. There's something else. The second gunshot vic. Banning Jefferson. Apparently he goes solely by a nickname. B.J."

Oh, Christ. "Bella's sixth date."

"Yeah. We didn't catch it earlier because B.J. wasn't on any of his IDs."

Jacob stared sightlessly out the laundry room window. "Bella wasn't the target today."

"No," Ethan agreed. "That would be Tyler Scott, date number three. And if he'd been hit, it'd have made three from her list of eight."

"Which puts me on the short list."

"Yeah," Ethan said grimly. "It does."

"I'll watch my back."

"See that you do. We're sending a squad car to your house, as well as to the other guys on the list. It leaves us strapped, but we have to stop this perp."

Jacob shut his phone and went into the kitchen. He grabbed a bottle of wine, two glasses and his laptop.

Bella had wandered into the living room, and was standing with her back to him in front of the huge picture window, looking out to the gentle rolling hills that lined his property. "It's so pretty out here." She turned and looked at him. "The land is beautiful. Are those your horses?"

"One's mine, one's my brother Wyatt's."

"The one in Afghanistan, flying for the air force."

"Yeah." Jacob set the laptop on the coffee table and poured the wine. "As for the land, I bought it a long time ago, before Santa Rey spread out this far. Back then, this place was a POS." He held out a glass of the wine.

She looked at it, then into his face. "Am I going to need that?"

His gaze didn't waver from hers. "Yes."

She sighed, then took it and sipped. "So. POS. Piece of shit?"

"Got it in one. I redid a room at a time, assisted by a brother or two. Took almost four years, but it's getting there."

She sipped some more wine, looking around her at the oversize, comfortably worn furniture. The only other adornments were a huge plasma TV on the wall and a variety of sports equipment.

"I keep meaning to put all that away," he said.

"Your house is big and warm and feels lived in, like a real home." She said this almost wistfully as she met his gaze. "Tell me what you've got, Jacob. I'm strong enough."

"I know."

"Then just put it out there, like ripping off a Band-Aid."

"All right." He took the wineglass from her fingers and set it aside, then pulled her closer, nudging her down to the couch. "Two things. The guy hit on the other side of town. His name is Banning Jefferson. But he goes by B.J."

She looked at him for a beat before it struck her. "Oh my God."

He took her hand. "He survived, Bella. Remember that. He's going to be okay."

"I need to see him."

"Tomorrow."

She stared at him, and he braced for a fight, but in the end, she simply nodded. "Thing two."

"Thing two." He looked into her eyes. "Today's shooting. You were with Tyler Scott. One of the eight."

"Yes, he came for dessert. He—" She gasped and covered her mouth. "The bullet was meant for him."

"It's likely."

She surged to her feet. "The others. We have to warn the others—"

He straightened and grabbed her before she could run for the door. "They're all being protected."

"And you?" She pulled back, gripping his arms in her hands, her fingers digging into his biceps. "You're in danger, too, just by being with me. You have to go. *Now.*"

"Bella—"

"Oh, God. You can't go, we're at your house. Okay, *I'll* go. I'll call a cab and—"

He pulled her back against his chest, wrapping his arms around her from behind. "I'm not sending you away."

"But—"

"We've got men on the shop, on all the dates, and now here, as well."

"Really?"

"Yes. And don't forget, the perp doesn't know where I live, my home address wasn't on my profile.

The guys were punking me, not trying to get me stalked and shot at."

"That's right," she murmured. "I keep forgetting you weren't on that date by your own choice."

"Maybe not at first." Turning her in his arms, he stroked a finger down her temple, tucking a strand of hair behind her ear. "But that changed pretty quickly."

She stared up at him. "When?"

"When a pretty, wild-haired brunette showed up, willing to have a first date that involved adventure seeking and getting her hair wet and her hands dirty."

She smiled at him, some of the panic leaving her eyes. "So what now, Jacob?"

"I want you to show me the profile you filled out, the one that the singles club used to line up your eight dates."

She moved back to the couch and opened his laptop. She waited until he leaned over her and typed in his password, then using his browser program, she accessed her e-mail and then opened a Word document.

"Bella?"

"It's pretty detailed."

He knew because he'd seen the one the guys had filled out for him. There'd been some innocuous questions, like favorite foods and colors. And some not-so-innocuous questions, like sexual likes and dislikes. And fantasies. The profile wasn't to be shared between any of the daters, only used to line up potential matches and, the club promised, would be destroyed afterward.

The guys at the P.D. had bullshitted their way through Jacob's. Since Bella hadn't had her so-called friends "help," most likely she'd answered truthfully, which meant that by allowing him to read her profile, he'd be reading her innermost thoughts and desires. It would be like peeling back the layers of the real Bella.

She made a sound that said "screw it" and thrust the laptop at him.

He looked at her, but had no idea what to say, so he began to read. Her favorite color was the color of the sun because it made her happy. Her favorite food was, surprise surprise, dessert of any kind. Her favorite clothes were anything that felt good and moved with her, she didn't care about labels or designers. Her favorite amusement ride was anything with speed. Her favorite thing she'd *not* yet done—fall in love.

He looked at her.

She lifted a shoulder. "I think I should try everything at least once, including love. You know, someday."

She was embarrassed, but for him he was struck by her honesty and bravado. Since she'd hate for him to point that out, he nodded, and ignoring his suddenly tight throat, quietly read on. The next section was a list of sexual preferences. She preferred one lover at a time, didn't mind toys when they were appropriate and didn't need a bed in order to get in the mood.

She'd left sexual fantasies blank.

"They should be individual to whoever you're with," she said.

He lifted his gaze to hers.

"Yes," she said.

"What?"

"You were going to ask if I have one for us. I do."

His body processed this faster than his brain. "Are you going to share?" he finally asked.

"You first," she said.

He felt a little thrown. A feeling he was starting to get used to around her. He knew now wasn't the time to be playful, but it felt like exactly the right time. They needed this. "Is this a show-and-tell sort of thing?"

"I think it just might be," she said, and for the first time since they'd gotten to his house, he smiled. "How bad do you want to know, Bella?"

She took the computer from his lap and set it aside. "Bad. Besides, you owe me."

"How do you figure?"

"I trusted you with my profile."

True. And, he realized, he trusted her. He, who because of his job and all he'd seen and done on that job, rarely trusted at all, trusted her to the bone after only a few days. He wasn't sure how he felt about that, but he wasn't quite jaded enough to let it go unappreciated. Pulling her onto his lap, he shifted her so that she was straddling him.

"Wait," she said, standing up and removing the jean shorts from beneath her dress. "More comfortable."

He was all for comfort.

She settled back on his lap, once again straddling him. "I like this sundress," he said. "It's the same one you wore after we went Jet Skiing." He ran his hands slowly up her smooth thighs, pushing up the hem as he went. "In my fantasy, you're not wearing anything beneath."

"That's it? That's your fantasy? That's…surprisingly tame."

"You didn't let me finish." His fingers glided higher on her thighs, and anticipation drummed between them. She was still covered by the hem of the sundress, but barely. "In my fantasy," he went on, his voice thick and hoarse to his own ears, "we go out on my bike, and the whole time we're riding, I can feel the heat of you, bare against me when you hug up close. You're covered from view to everyone else by the wide skirt of your sundress, only I know you don't have on panties."

Her breathing had definitely changed. Actually, he wasn't quite sure she was breathing at all, but the pulse at the base of her throat leaped wildly. "Then what?" she whispered.

"I take you out to dinner. While we're waiting for our food, I slip a hand beneath the table, under your dress. You're hot for me. You press yourself against my fingers, wanting more."

She opened her mouth a little, but nothing came out. Her eyes went glossy with arousal. He knew if he slid a hand beneath her dress right now, he'd find her hot and wet like in his fantasy. "We dance afterward. And every time I touch you, I'm reminded that you're bare-ass naked beneath the dress. Then you lean in and whisper in my ear that I'm making you wet, and I can't get you off the dance floor fast enough."

She drew in a shuddery gulp of air. "And then we make a run for the closest coat closet?"

"Mmm, good plan. We'll add that in. You'll scream my name, but no one but me will hear over the music."

"I want to make you lose control, too," she told him breathlessly. "You scream out my name, too."

He shook his head. "Guys don't scream. It's not manly."

She paused with a small smile. "Manly?"

"*My* fantasy."

"You're right," she said, pacifying him with a pat on the shoulder. "You can groan my name loudly. But hate to break it to you, it's still pretty tame."

"*Still* not finished." He ran a finger over her shoulder. "Someone keeps interrupting me."

"Sorry. Do go on."

"We get back on the bike and ride along the bluffs overlooking the ocean. There's no one around, so when your skirt blows up, you leave it."

He could tell by the way she nibbled on her lower lip that she liked that idea.

A lot.

"I reach back and feel you," he murmured, sliding both hands up to her hips, bringing the hem of her dress up, as well.

She was wearing a light blue silk thong. "You're completely exposed," he murmured. "And completely turned on by it. We pull over to the side of the road and—"

"Have some fairly acrobatic beneath-the-moon sex?" she asked hopefully, eyes dilated, voice husky.

"You have no patience." Giving in to temptation, he nudged her forward, lightly sinking his teeth into the spot where her neck met her shoulder, loving the shiver that racked her. "First I get off the bike and just look at you."

"Is my dress still hiked up to my waist?"

"Yeah. And you've unbuttoned the top part, too."

"No bra?"

"No bra, and when I pull the dress all the way off, you look up at me with a sexy little smile and slowly spread your legs."

"Like this?" And eyes on his, she did just that, opening her legs even farther over his.

Christ. "Yeah," he said hoarsely, watching the silk stretch tight over her mound. "And then you touch yourself. We both know anyone could walk by and see us at any time, but it doesn't stop you from opening my jeans and—"

"Wait a minute." She cocked her head. "I'm nearly buck-ass naked in the great outdoors, and you get to pull out just the essentials?"

"Yes, but the essentials are the important part." He wanted to laugh at the indignation on her face. "My fantasy," he reminded her.

"Men suck."

"Actually, you suck. It's what comes next in this scenario. Male Fantasy 101," he admitted. "But don't worry. Afterward, I lean you up against the bike, spread your legs, drop to my knees and return the favor until you're screaming my name again."

"You like that, the screaming thing."

"I do."

"Then what?" she asked.

"I turn you around, bend you over the bike and—"

"Let me guess. Make me scream." She shook her head. "You are such a guy." The mock annoyance wasn't fooling him. Her eyes were bright, she was having trouble breathing and her hands kept sweeping restlessly over his body, his shoulders, his abs…

"How about the water?" she asked. "Do we get in the water and go skinny-dipping?"

"Most definitely. And there's no male shrinkage at all."

She burst out laughing, and he grinned, loving the

sound. "In fact, you're so impressed with me, we do it again."

She snorted.

"And again," he said, gliding his hands along her smooth thighs.

"I wouldn't be able to walk." When his fingers got high enough to brush her panties, she closed her eyes and swallowed. "Or ride home."

"Fantasy," he reminded her, groaning when he stroked a finger over the taut silk and found it wet—

As if galvanized into action, she once again leveraged herself off him, evading his hands when he tried to stop her. "You're going to like this," she said. Lifting her hands, she untied the back of her halter dress, cupping the material to her breasts as it began to slide down.

She was right. He was liking this.

With a little smile, she slowly let it slip to her waist, exposing her bare breasts.

Her nipples had hardened into two tight peaks and his mouth went dry.

She slid her hands under the hem, giving him a quick peekaboo hint of that silk. Then she wriggled, and her hand reappeared with that blue silk, which she tossed over her shoulder.

Ah, yeah. He was liking this a lot.

"We're not on your bike," she murmured, slipping back onto his lap, straddling him. "But maybe we can improvise."

10

"I'M GOOD AT IMPROVISING," Jacob murmured in Bella's ear. The rough timbre of his voice made her shiver. It was true, she thought. He was really good.

Always.

He kissed her lips and she curled her fingers around his neck. She slid them into the soft, silky hair at the nape, making him let out a low sound that was half growl, half purr, as if her touch had suffused him with pleasure.

He wasted no time in once again pushing the dress up to her waist, but of course this time she was commando.

"Christ, look at you," he breathed reverently. "So pretty here." Lightly, he dragged his thumb over her wet flesh. "And here."

Her head fell back, mouth open as she tried to suck in some air, but someone had used it all. She tightened her fingers on his hair as he continued stroking her with that rough, callused thumb. His other hand gripped her hip, slowly rocking her against the hard bulge behind his button fly. Then his mouth joined the fray, hungry and demanding as it devoured hers.

It was all too much—and not enough. *"Jacob."*

"You feel so good, Bella." Sliding his hand around to cup her ass now, he pulled her harder against him, letting her experience just how good she made him feel.

She felt the same. Having him look at her like this had feminine power surging through her, and caused her pulse to throb in every erogenous zone in her body, of which there was suddenly so many. "Jacob—"

"Right here." His grip on her hips was tight, controlling as he ground against her rhythmically, causing the heat to spread. Her every muscle tightened, leaving her about an inch from orgasm.

"I can't get enough of you," he murmured, opening his mouth on her throat, still rocking, always rocking.

"Yes, but—" But she was going to go off far too quickly, she could feel it building within her even before he kissed and sucked and nibbled his way to her breasts.

"Oh God." She couldn't suppress the whimper, or slow the train down. Her mind was spinning with it, with the shocked realization of what he did to her, how he could make her so completely lose herself so that nothing, *nothing* else mattered but this.

Him.

His mouth fastened on her nipple, and with another helpless whimper, she arched her back as he continued to grind his erection hard between her legs, assaulting her senses, finding a spot deep inside her that no one else had touched. "You have to stop," she gasped, trying to pull free. "I'm going to—"

He merely tightened his grip, and then lightly clamped his teeth down on her nipple.

With a soft cry, she exploded—and lost her ability to see or hear anything over the roaring of the blood in her ears. When she could stop trembling and blink her vision clear, she pressed her face to his throat and moaned in embarrassment. "That was all your fault."

He slid his hands into her hair and lifted her face, his eyes scorching, his voice low and fierce. "I love the sounds you make when you come." He looked at her for a moment, then rose to his feet, effortlessly holding her. "Bed," he said, apparently done talking, preferring to move onto the doing portion of the evening. *"Now."* And he kissed her deep and wet while, without missing a beat or taking his tongue out of her mouth, he strode down the hall to his bedroom. At the side of his bed, he slowly let her slide down his body.

She opened his Levi's, pulled out just the "essentials" and stroked the thick, hard length of him. "Condom?"

He pulled one from his nightstand.

"In the name of fulfilling fantasies," she murmured, and with a last look in his eyes, turned from him and bent over the bed, knowing by the rough groan torn from his throat that he was enjoying the view. She felt his hands glide over her, gently murmuring in her ear when she jumped a little, soothing her with his touch as he pulled her back against him.

Then he slowly pressed into her, wrenching a sigh of pleasure from her and a deep groan from him. He went still a minute, letting her adjust to his size, then began stroking her in long, slow thrusts that had her trembling, once again on the very edge. His mouth was on her shoulder, one hand on her hip, the other gliding back and forth between her breasts, teasing her nipples into two hard aching points. Then his fingers trailed down her quivering belly, slipping between her thighs.

Gripping the blankets beneath her in two fists, Bella pressed her forehead into them as she gasped for air, making dark needy sounds that might have horrified her if she could have put a thought together. But Jacob's mouth was on her neck, his fingers strumming between her legs as he moved within her, and suddenly there was no thinking at all.

Behind her, Jacob groaned, struggling for control, a battle he lost as he followed her over, her name on his lips.

AFTERWARD, JACOB TOOK HER into the kitchen to raid his fridge. He wore his jeans, unbuttoned. Bella wore his shirt.

Also unbuttoned.

He handed her a bottle of water and she drank as if she hadn't had anything to drink for a week. "Your turn," he said, watching her throat convulse as she swallowed. Fascinated, he ran a finger down her throat to the center of her chest, changing directions to glide the pad of his callused thumb over her nipple. It hardened into a tight bead, and his body had a matching reaction. Jesus. He was never going to get enough of her. "Your fantasy next."

She looped her arms around his neck, sinking her fingers into his hair, making him practically purr. "You really want to know?"

He looked down into her face and felt something catch deep within him, and he knew in that moment that Ethan had been right.

He had it bad for her.

"I really do."

Tilting her head up, she met his gaze. "You show up at my place unannounced."

"Yeah?" His hands slid up the backs of her thighs, beneath the shirt.

"I open the door to you and tell you..." She affected a look of mock shame. "That I've been bad. Very, very bad."

"Mmm." His mouth was busy on the spot where

her neck met her shoulder, his fingers cupping and squeezing her sweet, bare ass. "How bad?"

She kissed one corner of his lips, then his jaw. His throat... "You have to cuff me."

His eyes drifted shut. "Do I?"

"Uh-huh... And then—" She licked his nipple.

"And then?" he managed to say.

"And then you exercise your authority," she whispered against his chest. "Because I've been so bad and all. I mean, *really* naughty."

He picked her up in tune to her surprised gasp, and carried her down the hall toward the bedroom, grabbing his cuffs on the way.

"Where are we going?" she asked breathlessly.

"To see just how bad you've been."

BELLA WOKE UP AND TOOK assessment. She was toasty warm, and someone had stolen all the bones in her body. She cracked open an eye.

She was face-first in Jacob's chest.

Not a bad place to be, as it was a world-class chest. She was snuggled up to his side with one leg and an arm thrown over him, hugging him to her like her own personal body pillow. The blankets were long gone. Only a sheet covered them, and it was pooled low at their waists. It was still dark outside but there was enough light slanting through his window from the predawn to see that Jacob was asleep.

As they'd not passed out until very late, and it was

debatable as to whether it was officially still very late or very early, she couldn't blame him.

He was on his back, far arm stretched above his head, the other wrapped around her. His face was turned toward hers, eyes closed, jaw whiskered in dark shadow. He looked younger, and extremely relaxed, as if maybe someone had stolen his bones, too, and the thought brought a knowing smile to her mouth. *She'd* put him in that state.

She could stare at him all night. Except she couldn't. She had to go.

He shifted, and drew in a deep breath. Eyes still closed, his arm tightened on her, and he pressed his face to the top of her head. "Mmm. Good way to wake up." His voice was sleep roughened and sexy as hell vibrating in her ear.

"Don't get stirred up," she said. "I have to get to the shop."

"Too late."

She crooked her neck and look down the length of him. Yep, it was too late. He was stirring.

Everywhere.

She watched as the sheet became an impromptu tent, and because she couldn't help herself, slid a hand beneath the fabric to wrap her fingers around him.

He groaned and covered her hand with his. "I like where this is going."

"It's not going anywhere. I have to start baking or we won't have anything to sell today. I'm not sure we'll have customers after all that's happened, but

I know Willow is going to be hoping for the best."
But because she couldn't help herself, she shoved the
sheet free and bent over him, kissing him on the very
tip of his most impressive erection.

It bobbed happily.

She gave one last sigh of regret and slipped out of
his arms and off the bed.

"That's just mean," he said as she padded off to
his bathroom. "Cruel and unusual punishment."

She was smiling when she turned on his shower,
smiling when she used his soap and pressed her nose
into her own arm to get as close to his scent as possible, smiling when she felt the door open behind
her.

And then she was pulled back against a solid, hard
chest. "No funny business," she warned him. "If you
behave, I'll meet you for lunch, but for right now, I've
got to go. Just cleaning up here, that's it, then I'll call
a cab."

"Hmm," he said noncommittally as his hands slid
up her soaped-up, slicked-up body and cupped her
breasts, his fingers grazing her nipples.

Her entire body quivered. "I mean it, Jacob."

"Fine. We'll do lunch."

"You mean, we'll do each other."

He grinned against her skin. "That, too, if you'd
like. I'll come to the shop, pick you up and feed you
first. Okay?"

"Mmm." It was all she could manage with one of
his hands on her breast, his other heading south—

She dropped the soap.

"Uh-oh," he murmured silkily. "Better get that."

When she bent over to get the soap, he sucked in a breath and gripped her hips. She felt him hard against her ass. "Jacob—"

"Just pretend I'm not even here," he said, both laughter and arousal in his voice.

"I'm only cleaning up," she repeated weakly, her body on high orgasm alert. Good Lord, it was crazy. They'd had each other so many times last night she'd lost count. How could she *still* want him like this? "I've really got to get going…"

"Oh, Bella." His voice was low and full of sexy promise. "You're going to get going. And coming…"

The words themselves almost edged her over. "The shop—"

"You're going to be late." He took the soap from her and directed her hands to the tile in front of her, gently kicking her feet farther apart as though he was about to frisk her. Then he slid a hand down her ass and groaned again. "*Very* late."

LATER THAT MORNING, JACOB was at his desk handling paperwork while reliving the morning's shower—look at him, multitasking—when Ethan stopped by.

"Just visited your girlfriend," Ethan said, annoying smirk in place. "She has the same just-been-thoroughly-laid look on her face that you do."

Jacob leaned back, lacing his hands over his abs. He was feeling far too mellow to put his fist in Ethan's mug, probably due to the just-been-thoroughly-laid feeling that was indeed running through his veins today.

Ethan dropped into a chair and stretched his legs. "We've put every spare man we've got on this case."

"I know. We're going to get him now."

Ethan nodded. "I've interviewed Willow, Trevor, all the neighboring shop owners and their employees, and all of the men Bella dated through the singles club."

"Except me."

"Except you. You haven't been contacted by the club since the date, right? Or by any of the other participants, other than Bella?"

"Nope."

"And no sense of being watched in any way?"

"No."

Ethan nodded. They both knew that once a cop, always a cop. If someone had been watching him, chances were Jacob would have noticed.

"Your club date with her was different than the others in two ways," Ethan said. "With everyone else, they had a meal or a drink, that was it. But with you, you changed venues and did quite a bit."

"Yeah. What's the second way it was different?"

Ethan waggled a brow. "You're the only one who slept with her. Did you know that was forbidden?"

"No, it wasn't."

"Okay, it wasn't," Ethan agreed. "But it was discouraged. So the question is, why you? Why did she sleep with you?"

"Thanks, man."

Ethan grinned. "I'm actually serious. It was out of character for her."

Truth was, Jacob didn't know why Bella had slept with him. All he knew was that from the moment they'd met, there'd been a spark—a physical, visceral spark—and it was still there, every time he saw her.

Every.

Single.

Time.

"You've kept seeing her," Ethan said. "Not that anyone could blame you. But she hasn't made a move to see any of the others again."

"So?"

"So are you exclusive already?"

"And that's pertinent to the case how?"

"Oh, it's not. Just wondering what that sweet little thing sees in you. I mean, look at her. She's warm and funny and sexy as hell. You on the other hand are grumpy, usually scowling, and I'm having a hard time imagining you bringing the funny or the sexy." He rose lithely to his feet when Jacob's eyes narrowed, and wisely moved to the door.

"Ethan?"

"Yeah?"

"I can't see a rhyme or reason to the order in which the eight of us are being targeted."

Ethan shook his head. "Me, neither. Just be careful out there," he warned. "And though I don't believe she's the target, I've advised Bella to do the same."

At lunchtime, Jacob shoved the reports he'd been working on aside and left the building. He was halfway to Edible Bliss when he was called to check on a material witness for a case he was building involving the identity-theft ring.

Thanks to an uncooperative witness and an unhappy victim, by the time Jacob was back on the road again, it was nearly two.

Bella had probably eaten lunch without him long ago.

Still, he headed over there, needing to see her. It had nothing to do with his own emotions and feelings, he assured himself, and everything to do with what Ethan had said.

She needed to be careful.

Something bad had happened each day for three days running, and he just wanted to lay his eyes on her—and maybe his hands—and know she was okay.

Over the years he'd had hundreds of cases, and had met countless people he'd worried about in the scope of the job. But this wasn't just the job. This was personal.

Almost too much so.

He parked his bike in the back lot next to the

squad car assigned to the shop, nodding to the cop inside. It was Tom Kennedy, a rookie of less than a year. They spoke for a minute, and when Tom said he hadn't had lunch yet, Jacob told him to take off and grab something, that he'd watch the place until he got back.

Jacob stepped up to the kitchen door, wanting to take a quick peek inside before he made a complete check around the perimeter of the building.

Bella was alone, bustling around in tune to the sound system, which she had blaring Radiohead. She wore a pair of tiny denim shorts, an oversize white men's T-shirt knotted in the small of her back, a siren-red apron, and matching red high-tops on her feet. That made him smile.

Hell, *she* made him smile.

Her wild hair was piled up on top of her head, a few wispy tendrils escaping, sticking to her damp temples. He knew just how that damp skin would taste, and he felt himself stir with arousal just looking at her.

Then he pictured her in that apron, and nothing else.

Christ, he needed help. If he had ever doubted the necessity of removing himself from the case, this moment made it irrefutable.

She hadn't seen him yet. She was singing to herself as she cleaned the countertop, the motion making her hips rock back and forth.

And making him ache.

Christ, he was gone. Completely gone over her. He hoped she'd decide to come out and get some air, but clearly she was getting ready to close up. Leaning against the doorjamb, he stood there with a ridiculous grin on his face, just soaking her in. He figured he could probably stand there and watch her all damn day long and not get tired of it, but then she vanished into the front room of the shop, where he could no longer see or hear her.

And he had a job to do first before he went inside. He straightened up to get on with it just as the hair on the back of his neck suddenly stood up. He jerked around at the exact moment the shot rang out.

He jerked again at the impact, and fire burned through him.

He really hated getting shot.

He opened his mouth to yell a warning to Bella, since he knew she couldn't hear a thing over her music, but nothing came out. His last thought at he hit the ground was that at least he wasn't holding a bouquet of flowers.

11

BELLA MOVED TO THE front door of the shop, locked it, then looked over the freshly installed window. Remembering the reason for that had a shiver racking her as she flipped the Closed sign. She moved to the iPod dock in the closet and hit the power button, and in the sudden silence, another shiver, this one of dread, raced up her spine. She stepped out of the closet and looked around for the cause.

Everything looked normal.

Then Willow's face appeared in the front door's window, and Bella near fell back on her butt in surprise.

"Sorry," Willow said when Bella had opened the door for her. "Forgot my key and my purse." She frowned. "I don't know where my head is."

"I do. It's on the shootings, and the fact that we had half our usual customers today."

Willow sighed. "Yeah. That's it."

Her hair was spiked straight up and out today, like Cher in her seventies Oscar run. She was wearing retro derby gear complete with polyester shorts and a green-and-white rugby top. The only thing missing was a pair of skates and the pads. "You're wearing your mom's clothes again."

"Yeah, I love her closet. I'm going to stay there again tonight. There's an extra couch…"

"Thanks. I'll let you know."

Hands on hips, Willow's eyes narrowed as she studied Bella. "You're eating your short-crust pastry."

Bella looked down at the pastry in her hands and sighed. "Had so much left over today. And it's good."

"It's great," Willow corrected. "It's soft and flaky and *perfect*. But according to you, it also goes right to your hips."

"You forgot your purse and keys due to stress. I'm eating due to stress. We're quite the pair." Bella sighed again and tossed the pastry into the trash.

"Well, Jesus, if you were going to throw it away…" Willow looked wistfully at the trash can.

"Don't you dare." They moved into the kitchen, where Bella gave her a new one from the leftovers bin, and Willow happily bit into it.

Bella shook her head. "I hate that you can eat like this and stay as skinny as a rail."

Willow grinned and took another pastry. "Good genes." She cocked her head and her smile faded. "There's something else wrong. Aw, honey. Is it Sexy Cop?"

"No. Yes. I don't know." She shook it off. "It's nothing. He was supposed to meet me for lunch and didn't. No biggie."

"He's got an important job. He probably just got held up."

"Yes. Maybe." But maybe not. Maybe he'd decided their casual fun was over.

"He doesn't seem like the sort of man to play with a woman's feelings," Willow said quietly. "And anyway, I've seen him look at you. He'd never play with you like that. Something came up. He'll call."

"Yeah."

"You keep going down that path," Willow said, grabbing her purse, "and you're going to be insane by the end of the day. I'm going to the movies. Trevor's driving. Come with us?"

"Not today, thanks."

Willow gave her a fast hug. "You're just afraid because you're feeling more than you meant to, because you're falling for him."

Bella squeezed her eyes shut. "Maybe."

"Don't worry, Bell, I think he means to catch you."

And then she was gone, out through the dining area and the front door, and with a sigh, Bella locked up. For the tenth time, she pulled out her cell phone.

No missed call.

Fine. He hadn't called. That was fine.

You're falling for him. Willow's words echoed in her head. They were a scary truth. *Her* scary truth, because she *was* falling.

But was she the only one? Hard to tell. But if so, that was okay. He'd said casual. It wasn't his fault that she hadn't managed to keep it that way. She'd get herself together.

She would.

She sagged a little, feeling the ache behind her ribs that showed her up as a big, fancy liar. With a shake of her head, she turned off the lights, grabbed her key and went to push open the back door, but it got stuck on something. She pushed a little harder, and when it moved enough for her to squeeze out, she nearly tripped over—

A body.

He was on his side facing away from her. Dark hair, buff arms, broad shoulders, blood pooling beneath him on the ground—

Oh, God.

This wasn't just any body, this one was as familiar to her as her own.

With a groan, Jacob shifted, and she stepped over him and dropped to her knees with a shocked sob. *"Jacob!"* His shirt was light blue, so she could clearly see the hole in his shoulder, and the blood pumping from it. Panic clenched her hard in the gut, and she ripped off her T-shirt, wadding it up to press it to his wound as she whipped out her cell phone and pounded 911.

He rolled to his back, face tight in a grimace as she gave the information to emergency dispatch.

"Goddamn," he said through his teeth when she was done and pressed harder on the wound. "That hurts."

She slid a hand beneath his head to move it to her lap, and her fingers came away bloody. "You must have hit your head."

"Well, that's a relief." He was staring up at her and blinking rapidly. "Explains why there's four of you." He closed his eyes. "Get inside and stay away from the windows."

"What? I'm not leaving you!"

"Goddammit, Bella. The shooter could still be out here somewhere."

She lifted her head and looked around, heart pumping so hard she could scarcely breathe. "No one's out here."

"Did it go through?"

"What?"

"The bullet. Did it go through?"

She let out a breath and looked him over. Hole in the front. Gently she leaned over him so she could see the back.

God.

God, there was so much blood. "Yes," she said shakily. "It went straight through."

"That's good." His eyes were a little glazed and fixed on what was right in front of his face—her chest. "Nice bra."

She made a sound that was a half laugh, half sob, and applied more pressure.

"Oh, shit," Jacob rasped through his teeth.

"I'm sorry. You're bleeding so much."

"Call Ethan. Have him tell Tom his lunch break's over."

Again she used her cell. Onlookers were starting to trickle into the parking lot, one of whom brought her a shawl to wrap around herself. Two of the adjacent shop owners were there, too, and several people that Bella didn't know, all standing a respectful distance back.

She heard sirens. "They're coming."

He didn't move or open his eyes and she gripped him tight. "Jacob!"

"Shh," Jacob whispered. "He's sleeping."

"No. Stay with me," she said fiercely, leaning down to put her face right in his. "Don't you dare leave me."

"Bella," he said softly, sounding pained. He squeezed her hand. "I'm not going anywhere."

"Okay, then."

He didn't say anything more, but she could see his chest rising and falling. Breathing. Breathing was good.

The ambulance pulled into the lot and everything happened in super speed then. She was pulled free of Jacob, who was quickly assessed, his vitals taken and an IV started. She heard the EMT report to the hospital that they had a thirty-two-year-old male with a through-and-through GSW to the shoulder, vitals stable, possible slight concussion.

She never took her eyes off Jacob. He was clearly woozy, but he'd been able to give his name, age, the time and place. That had to be good, she told herself.

Then he was loaded up.

She tried to go with him, but another EMT detained her, gaze running over her gently as he assessed her to make sure the blood all over her wasn't hers. By the time it was determined she was fine, the ambulance with Jacob had left.

Fine. She knew just where the hospital was, since on her first week in Santa Rey she'd cut her finger with her paring knife and had required three stitches. She needed a shirt anyway, and she had to lock up, and she had to—

"Bella."

She turned and found a grim-looking Ethan, and nearly lost it at the familiar face.

Right. She had to talk to the police.

Yet again.

"Oh, Christ," he said when he got a good look at her. "Were you hit?"

"No, it's Jacob's blood."

He backed her into the kitchen, keeping a tight grip on her until she sat in a chair. Without a word, he went to the refrigerator and got her a bottle of water. "Drink," he said, and went to the sink to wet a towel.

"Someone shot him," she said softly.

"I know." Gently he pulled the shawl off her, then ran the towel over her arms. He rinsed it out, then handed it back to her, presumably so that she could do her own torso. "What did you see?" he asked.

"Nothing. I saw nothing. I got a sort of hinky feeling, and I shrugged it off." She shook her head. "Willow came back for her purse—"

"Willow was here?"

"Yes, briefly. After she left, I came to the back door here to leave, and nearly tripped over him. He was just lying there." Her hand was shaking so badly she couldn't drink. "And I'm shaking. I never shake."

He shrugged out of his shirt and wrapped it around her. "Are you going to take me to the station again?" she asked him.

"I'm not a complete asshole. I'm going to wait for you to collect yourself, then I'm going to drive you to the hospital to see him."

She lifted her head and met his gaze. "You're worried about him, too."

A muscle ticked in his jaw. "Yeah."

She stood up. "Consider me collected."

He looked her over as if to make his own assessment, then he reached for her hand and took her to his car.

<u>12</u>

GETTING SHOT SUCKED. Being X-rayed and MRI'd sucked. Lying in a hospital bed sucked.

Jacob kept his eyes closed because somehow he hurt less that way. What else sucked? he wondered. Oh, yeah, wearing a stupid hospital gown with his ass hanging out—

At the slight rustle at his side, he gave up the pity party and opened his eyes.

The room immediately started spinning wildly. Thank you, morphine.

The lights were low. He could hear the soft muted sounds of monitors and sensed activity just outside his door, but inside his room, all was fairly quiet.

Turning just his head, he came face-to-face with Bella. She was sitting in a chair by his bed, hunched over the raised mattress, head down on her folded arms.

Given her slow, even breathing, he concluded she

was sleeping. Her hair was a wild, riotous wreck. He was fairly certain there was blood in it, and his heart picked up speed until he realized it was probably his. She wore a man's shirt, not his, shoved up to the elbows, and with her face turned to the side, he could make out the very faint tracks of whisker burns on the underside of her jaw.

Those were his.

She was a quiet, tousled, clearly exhausted mess, and maybe it was the fact that he was as high as a kite, but no one had ever looked better to him.

The door opened behind her, but thanks to what he knew from experience was a combination of a severe adrenaline letdown and an emotional exhaustion, she didn't so much as stir as his brother Austin walked in.

He and Jacob were only a year and a half apart, and on a normal day, when one of them wasn't lying in a hospital bed trussed up with bandages and on some good mind-altering drugs, they could have passed for twins. Dark hair, matching dark eyes and a tendency for walking headfirst into trouble.

"Just talked to your doctor—" Austin glanced at Bella, raised a brow, then silently sat on the other side of Jacob's bed. "That her?"

"Who?"

"The woman you went out with, the one you dropped off the face of the planet for over the past few days."

Jacob felt the stupid smile cross his lips and

couldn't do a damn thing about it. "Her name is Isabella Manchelli—Bella. She works at Edible Bliss. She's a pastry chef and a friend."

"Great," Austin said. "But none of that answered my question."

"Keep it down, she's asleep."

Austin raised a brow. He looked Bella over, taking in the wild hair, the way her mouth was slightly open, and he smiled. "She's cute."

Bella shifted, turned her head over to the other side, and in the process, lifted up briefly enough to reveal more blood in her hair.

Austin's smile faded. "Tell me she's not hurt."

"It's my blood. Tell me what the doctor said."

"X-ray and MRI were negative, no bullet fragments. Mild concussion. You're going to hurt like a son of a bitch, but while you're in here you get morphine. You're probably going to be woken every two to three hours, but the good news is that the nurse on duty is pretty damn hot. Still, the next time you're going to be stupid enough to stand on the back stoop of a woman who tends to get her men shot at, the least you could do is wear a vest." He paused and looked over Bella again. "So you're dating her?"

"Why?"

"Why? Because you met her through a singles club. Seems kind of cheesy, man."

"Should I have met her on a bar stool like you meet your one-night stands?"

"So she's a one-night stand?"

Their gazes met and Jacob sighed. "I don't know. I can't think straight. Are you on the merry-go-round or am I?"

Cord entered the hospital room at a dead run, or more accurately, a limping run on a leg that hadn't quite healed yet. Eyes a little wild, he stopped short and gripped the doorjamb. "You were shot."

"Yeah," Jacob said.

"You're breathing."

"Yeah."

"And wasted," Austin added.

Cord let out a slow, careful breath, then sank to a chair. "I didn't get details, just a text from Mr. Talkative here, and I—" He broke off with a shake of his head and put a hand to his heart. "Christ, man."

"I'm okay," Jacob said. "Though you've split into two. You need some help."

Cord just stared at him. "Christ," he finally said again. He hadn't been back from his last overseas mission all that long and was still a little jumpy. "What I need is whatever you're on." He turned to Austin. "Prognosis?"

"Hard head still intact, and expected to make a full recovery," Austin told him. "He's going to be okay, Cord."

Cord nodded but still looking shaken, leaned his head back to the wall.

Austin turned to Jacob with a raised brow. "Why don't you tell baby brother here how you're on, what, date number three? With the same woman.

That woman, in fact." He gestured to a still-sleeping Bella.

That seemed to knock Cord out of his own thoughts. "She must be a walking fantasy or something." He cocked his head. "Kinda hard to tell with the crazy hair."

"Fantasy," Jacob repeated, brain fuzzy. "We knocked out fantasy number one. Need to move on to fantasy number two."

That had both Austin and Cord giving each other a speculative look. "What's fantasy number two?" Austin wanted to know.

"Her in her apron and nothing else."

Cord grinned, the hauntedness and hollowness gone from his gaze. "Those must be some good drugs."

Austin took in Jacob's expression and shook his head. "Oh, Christ."

"What?" Jacob asked, his eyes at half mast now. They were closing on him without his permission.

"You've got that look, the same stupid, love-struck look that Cord had right before he admitted he'd fallen for Lexi."

"Hey," Cord said. "True, but—hey."

"I'm pretty sure I'm just high," Jacob said in his own defense.

"I actually hope that's true," Austin said. "Because if you fall, too, that leaves me hanging out here all alone, and even I can't handle all the single women in town by myself."

Cord grinned. "You can try."

"You still have Wyatt," Jacob said, reminding Austin that their other brother was still single. "He'll be home soon enough."

A shocked silence echoed between them as Jacob's words said sank in. "Wait a minute," he said. "I didn't mean that I *am* falling."

They all turned their heads to stare at a still deeply sleeping Bella, and Jacob's gut tightened. His heart tightened, too. Typically when he looked at her, his dick tightened, as well, but nothing there. Damn meds.

A little snuffling whimper escaped from Bella, and Jacob stroked her arm with his hand. "Shh," he said. "It's okay now."

Her frown smoothed out and she let out a shuddery breath.

And just like that, his dick twitched. Good to know he was in fine working order after all.

Austin was staring at him. "You're soft around her."

"Soft?" He begged to differ.

"You know what I mean." He looked at Bella and then shook his head. "What does she see in you?"

Jacob sighed. "Thanks for coming by."

"But go away?"

"That'd be great."

WHEN JACOB WAS RELEASED from the hospital late the next evening, Bella was waiting to take him home.

She'd spent the night with Willow at her mom's, then gone back to her place to shower and change, and now had a purse full of happy pills and two pages of doctor's instructions as she slid her arm around Jacob for the walk out.

"I'm not an invalid," he said, smiling down at her.

He'd been smiling a lot since he'd started the happy pills. He'd smiled at the nurse, and she'd dropped her supplies. He smiled at his brother, who was currently on his other side helping Bella get him to the car, and Austin just shook his head and said, "You're a sap."

"Love you, too, man," Jacob said, making Austin laugh.

Austin turned to Bella. "Take care of the idiot, will you?"

"Plan on it."

And now the "idiot" was smiling at her as she drove him home, making her heart catch in her throat.

Her life had turned into a *Law & Order* episode, and he was smiling at her.

God. She could hardly bear to think about what had happened to him, or how much worse it could have been.

Ethan and most of the P.D. were on this case, she told herself. They would find the shooter, Ethan had promised. They would take care of it.

She knew it, she believed it.

She just hoped they'd do so before anyone else got hurt.

At Jacob's house, she guided him to the couch, removed his shoes and sank back on her heels to look up at him.

"You stopping at the shoes?" he asked, and wriggled his toes.

"Yes. Why?"

"I'm not comfortable. I want to be in sweats."

She dutifully pulled off his socks.

"And?" he asked with a sweet grin that was so amiable and easygoing—unlike his usual stoic, tough, badass self—she laughed. "You are feeling no pain today, Detective." But she obliged him by unbuttoning his shirt and carefully easing it off his shoulders, working around the splint and sling his left shoulder was immobilized with. At the sight of all the thick bandages, her mirth faded.

He hadn't required surgery—a miracle. Nothing vital had been hit.

Another miracle.

He was a walking miracle...

"And?" he murmured again, arching a brow.

She looked at his jeans. Levi's, button fly. She ran her finger over his corrugated abs, which contracted beneath her touch. She popped the top button and felt him harden beneath the denim, and then it was her turn to arch a brow.

"He's excited to see you," Jacob explained.

"You say that like it's been so long," she murmured,

crawling between his long legs and leaning in so that she could rest her head on his stomach. "It's only been a day and a half."

"He's greedy when it comes to you."

With a soft laugh, she turned her face and nuzzled his belly button. His skin was silky smooth, with the ripple of hard sinew just beneath. "I think this is my favorite spot on you."

He was lying back against the couch, his eyes at half mast, his long, thick lashes shielding his thoughts. He brought his good hand up to her hair. "I was hoping your favorite spot was down a little."

She stroked the spot he was talking about, and he let out a sigh, which turned into a ragged groan when she dragged her tongue south to the Levi's waistband, snaking it just beneath.

"Christ, Bella." His hand tightened in her hair. He kept his head back, his eyes now closed, throat exposed. She watched his Adam's apple as he swallowed.

"You have no idea what you do to me," he murmured.

She eyed the growing bulge behind the button fly. "Oh, I think I do... You know, you might be right about my favorite body part. Let me take a look." She popped open the rest of his buttons, and he sprang free. In the same way she'd nuzzled his belly, she leaned in and pressed her face against him, then gave him a kiss.

His breathing had accelerated, but other than that,

the rest of his long body was stone still, clearly waiting for her next move.

"You do realize," she whispered, her lips brushing him with each word, "this isn't doctor recommended."

"He said I should go with what feels good. Trust me, Bella. You feel good."

"Well, stop me if anything causes you any pain." She let her tongue dart out and run the hard length of him.

"You're not hurting me." His voice was raw. "You're *killing* me. But, Christ, please don't stop."

In less than three minutes, she had him quivering, alternating between swearing and begging. In two more, he was panting, boneless and completely sated.

"You okay?" she whispered, sitting back on her heels.

"If I was any more okay, I'd float out of here and into bed."

She smiled. "I'll help you." She got him down the hall and onto the mattress, and he lay there, eyes closed, color a bit ashen. She'd never rebuttoned his jeans, and she already knew he was commando beneath them, but she still couldn't help but stare as he one-armed them down his legs and kicked them away.

She'd had her mouth on every single inch of that glorious, gorgeous body and still, she wanted him.

She was afraid she always would. "You hungry? Thirsty? Need anything?"

He made an almost inaudible negative sound.

She covered him with a blanket and moved to leave the room, but, eyes still closed, he reached out and unerringly snagged her wrist.

Seemed he was down for the count but still in complete control of his instincts. "You okay?" she asked.

"It's late."

"Yes. So?"

"So…" He tugged, and with a gasp, she sank down beside him on his good side.

"Jacob, careful—"

"Don't drive home this late, don't go be by yourself."

"I won't be alone. There's still a man on the shop."

"Just stay."

"But you need to rest. You're not up for—"

"I won't be able to rest if I'm worried about you, and if you go back there, I'll worry."

She went still for a long moment, her eyes closed, chest aching, wishing he'd say, "Stay with me because I want you to."

She'd told herself she didn't need to hear that from him but she did.

God, she did. She needed to hear it from someone in her life, someone who wasn't family, who didn't have to say it.

"You should know," she finally whispered to him in the dark, her hand caught in his. "I'm...afraid. Of you. Of me. I don't do things like this, Jacob. I don't let guys in. I like to keep my options open, I like to be free to up and leave whenever. And I'm due to leave." She paused, then decided what the hell. She'd already anted up, might as well play out the round. "But even with an entire lifetime of experience of keeping my emotions in check, with you I let go. I let go and let myself feel, all in a matter of days, which is where the terror comes in." She let out a low laugh, and dropping to her knees beside the bed, she hugged his hand to her chest, pressing her face into his good shoulder. "Fact is," she murmured, "I think I'm beginning to maybe, a little bit, fall for you."

He said nothing.

Lifting her head, she looked into his face.

His eyes were closed, his face relaxed. "Jacob?"

Nothing. The happy pills had done their job and knocked him out.

13

JACOB WOKE UP SLOWLY, groggy and disoriented. He blinked at the ceiling. It was *his* ceiling. He was in his own bed.

That was good.

He closed his eyes, trying to figure out what he remembered last.

He'd been shot.

Yeah, he remembered that really well. He remembered Bella holding his head on her lap and crying softly over him.

He remembered her begging him not to go to sleep, and remembered staring into her eyes and wanting to promise her anything, his motorcycle, his bank account, his life, if only she wouldn't cry.

He didn't remember the ambulance ride or the E.R., but he remembered Bella sleeping at his side, and Austin and Cord coming to see him, the two of them looking at him with dark, worried eyes, and

Austin saying that if Jacob was going to be stupid enough to stand on the back stoop of a woman who tended to get her men shot, then the least he could do was wear a vest.

Point taken.

He needed protection when it came to Bella. Unfortunately the kind of protection he needed was a heart guard, and that hadn't been invented yet.

But he was home now...

How had he gotten here?

His bedroom door opened and Bella slid in, carrying a pitcher and a glass. She set them down very quietly then turned to smooth his covers, and nearly jerked right out of her skin when she saw that his eyes were open.

"Oh! You're awake! Are you in pain? Do you need—"

"You. I need you." With his good hand, he tugged her down to the bed. The shift nearly killed him, but he sucked in a breath and managed a smile. "You're a sight for sore eyes."

She visibly softened and cupped one side of his jaw, pressing her mouth to the other side. "Right back at you. Do you need another pain pill?"

"Yes, but don't give me one. I can't even remember getting here."

Her eyes widened. "You don't remember the...um, couch?"

He went still as it came back, her kneeling between his spread legs, her mouth on him, and the memory had pleasure suffusing his body. "I thought that was just a really great dream." He met her gaze. "Thank you, by the way. But I still don't remember getting into bed."

She nodded and looked away, and he'd swear that was relief crossing her features. He stroked a thumb over the backs of her fingers. "What did I do, Bella?"

"Nothing."

"Did I say anything to upset you?"

"No, nothing like that." She sagged a little. "It was me, okay? *I* said something I shouldn't have." She bit her lower lip and stared at him.

He blinked. "What was it?"

She groaned and pressed her forehead to his good shoulder. "Never mind. Are you thirsty? I brought you water, the doctor said not to let you get dehydrated."

"Bella—"

"Here." She sat up at his hip and poured him a glass.

He lifted a hand to her wrist and she shook her head. "Please?"

He looked at her for a long moment, then nodded his reluctant agreement to let the subject go. She held the glass to his lips and, looking over the edge at her, amused, he sipped.

"Hungry?" she asked. "I can cook you up some breakfast before I have to go."

He smiled. "In your apron?"

She arched a brow.

"Sorry. That was fantasy number two. We never got to it."

"You have a fantasy about me in an apron?"

He shook his head, feeling a little fuzzy. "I'm sorry. It's a guy thing."

"Huh." She got off the bed. "Breakfast. I'll get it." And then she was gone.

He went back to studying the ceiling. *Way to go, Madden. You had her in here, warm and smiling, then you scare her off with some stupid, sexist, subservient-male fantasy—*

She came back into the room, and holy shit. If he hadn't been lying down, he'd have fallen. She was wearing a black bra and matching panties, low on her hips and sexy enough to put him into heart-attack danger. She'd created an apron out of one of his kitchen towels and used another to create a little cap on her head.

"At your service, sir," she murmured throatily, giving him a little curtsy. "What can I get you?"

"What are you doing?"

"Well, I was going for a French-maid thing, but I can't pull off the accent."

He could only stare at her as she sashayed across the room and sat perched at his hip with a small, warm smile. Leaning over him, she lightly brushed her lips to his.

He was afraid he was drooling. "God, Bella," he said on a low, baffled, bewildered laugh. "I—"

Austin walked into the bedroom and stopped short with a choked breath at the sight of Bella sitting on Jacob's bed, leaning over him in nothing but her underwear. "Um," he said brilliantly.

"Jesus, Austin," Jacob snapped as Bella squealed and dived under the covers with him, hiding her face in his armpit. "Get out."

"Sorry," Austin said, then just stood there with a broad grin on his face. "I came to see if you needed anything, but I can see that you are being extremely well taken care of."

From beneath the covers, Bella squeaked again.

Austin just continued to grin like a jackass. "Fantasy number two. *Nice.*"

Still out of sight, Bella punched Jacob in his good arm. *"You told him?"*

Jacob shook his head. "No. I—"

"Yeah," Austin said. "You told us at the hospital. Don't be mad, Bella," he said to the lump under the sheet. "We totally took advantage of him being high."

While Jacob was appreciating—and loving—the feeling of Bella wearing only her panties and bra all pressed up against him and squirming, he figured he had about three seconds to get his brother out of here before she killed him. "Austin?"

"Let me guess. Get the hell out?" With a grin, he said, "Going. But next time you play dress up, you really should lock the door."

"Maybe next time you should knock."

"And miss out on all the fun?" With a laugh, Austin turned toward the door. "I'll be in the kitchen making myself something to eat. Loudly, so I can't hear you two do your thing."

Jacob decided it was worth the pain and reached for the phone on the nightstand to chuck it at his brother's head, but Austin laughed again and hastily shut the door behind him.

Leaving a stunned and awkward silence.

For a beat, the only thing visible of Bella was a few strands of wild hair, then suddenly she was in motion, leaping out of the bed, her makeshift cap all askew, the apron half on, half off, one of her bra straps slipped to her elbow.

She looked hot as hell.

"So," he said. "Where were we?"

She whirled, eyes reflecting her disbelief. "You have got to be kidding me."

"He said he'd make lots of noise so he couldn't hear you—"

"Oh, my God." She hauled open his closet door. Her underwear was riding up in back, giving him a heart-attack-inducing view. "He said he'd make lots of noise so he couldn't hear the *two* of us. He didn't specify *me*."

"Honey," Jacob said with a smile.

She went still, then turned on him in her half-naked glory, eyes narrowed. "Honey, what? And be careful here, because it seems like you might be suggesting that only one of us makes a lot of noise in bed."

Jacob wisely wiped the smile off his face. By the look on hers, he wasn't entirely successful.

She yanked off both the cap and the apron and helped herself to a pale blue button-down from his closet. It came to her thighs and she looked just as hot as she had in only her underwear. "Sweats," she demanded.

"Third drawer down." He pointed to his dresser.

"I can't help it if I'm...noisy," she said, helping herself to a pair of dark blue air force sweats that dragged on the floor. She pulled them up with a hip shimmy that made his eyes cross.

"Bella?"

"What?"

"I love the noises you make," he said. "Especially when I'm—"

"Shh!" She rolled the sweats at her waist a handful of times, shot him another indecipherable look and stalked barefoot to the door.

"Where are you going?"

"I promised Willow I'd pick up some supplies and fill a couple of restaurant orders."

"Bella, I don't want you to go into the building—"

"I know. But they have a unit watching the place, and they said it was okay. I'll be very careful. I just have some things to take care of."

"I thought I was one of the things you were going to take care of."

She slid him a bemused look. "Are you saying you need me to stay, or you want me to stay?"

Okay, he knew a trick question when he heard one. Problem was, he didn't know which was the right answer, the one that would have her stepping out of his clothes and sliding into his bed.

And this wasn't about fulfilling a fantasy. He really needed to keep her here so that he would know she was safe. But his mind was fuzzy with meds, and the emotion he'd almost let slip right before Austin had walked in. If his brother hadn't shown up and Jacob had said, "I love you," Bella already would have gone running for the door. And running from him. "Um…"

At his lack of response, something came and went in her eyes, and he got the very bad feeling that he'd somehow hurt her.

"I think Austin can handle anything you need," she said.

"Yeah, but he won't look nearly as good in that apron." Even to his own ears, his words rang hollow. Why couldn't he just say what he was thinking? Jesus, he was pathetic.

She stared at him, then stared at her feet a long moment. "Nice try." Leaning in, she kissed his jaw. "Bye, Jacob."

She was going to walk away, and his heart skipped

a beat. "Hey," he said, snagging her hand. "Forget the apron thing. I shouldn't have—"

"It's okay. It's not that."

"Then—"

"Forget it. It's all good." She smiled, but it didn't quite make it to her eyes, and he knew for sure that he'd hurt her.

Dammit. "Wait—"

But she was already gone from the room. He lunged out of the bed after her, and gray spots danced in his vision from getting up too fast, dropping him to all fours, where he struggled to stay conscious. It took a long thirty seconds for the spots to fade before he could stagger to his feet. He stumbled down the hall in time to hear a car rev, and whipped his front door open. It wasn't until he felt the chilly morning air that he realized he was naked.

"Hey," Austin said, coming around the corner from the kitchen. "Do you want eggs— Holy shit, man. Put some clothes on."

"Why did you let her go?"

"Um, because they frown on unlawful detainment in this country?"

"She left upset."

Austin gestured to Jacob's nudity. "Yes, well, have you seen you?"

"Austin?"

"Yeah?"

"Shut up." Jacob took his sorry, naked ass back to bed, where he called Ethan and asked him to double the watch on Edible Bliss. He called Bella, who surprise surprise, didn't pick up. "Please come back out here when you're done," he said to her voice mail. "And call me when you're leaving the shop, okay?" Then he laid back down, pensive and unsettled, knowing he'd in all likelihood just ruined the best thing that had ever happened to him.

BELLA WAS DROPPING OFF the supplies in the shop's kitchen when Willow came in. "Honey, you should be playing doctor with Sexy Cop."

"I wanted to get us set up for when we reopen."

"Or you wanted to outrun your guilt."

"How do you know I feel guilty?"

"Honey."

Bella shook her head. "It's not that. I mean, I feel…" She closed her eyes. "I am devastated over the shootings, but I know it's not my fault. I'm—"

Willow raised a brow.

And Bella let out a long breath. "I'm in this fight with myself. My head and gut are telling me to go, to leave town and move on, but—"

"But your heart is telling you to stick."

"I don't know." Bella had to purposely draw in another breath and let it out again. "Maybe. A little. Santa Rey was supposed to be nothing more than a pin on my map. A quick stop. But—"

"But you want to grow roots."

Bella had to smile. "I like the finishing-my-sentences thing."

"Yeah? See if you can finish this one for me. You're in the shop, worried about my business, maybe risking your life to be here instead of nursing your man because…?"

"Because he's *not* my man. Because he doesn't know what he wants. I mean, he wants me, but he doesn't *want* me."

"Huh?"

Bella rolled her eyes. "Forget it. Even I don't understand me."

"Hey, I saw him kiss you. Lord, I need a cold shower every time I think about it. Yeah, he wants you bad, but it's more than lust. You're not alone in this."

Bella wanted Willow to be right, but the fear of not being loved and accepted was an old one. Logic didn't seem to be able to make a dent against it. Hell, even stone-hard facts didn't have a chance against an irrational decades-old fear like hers.

Willow helped her put things away. Afterward, the cop on duty escorted Willow to her car where she planned on heading to her mom's, with Bella agreeing to follow as soon as she put a bag together.

The cop then escorted Bella upstairs, where she took a quick moment to grab her mail, going still when she came to a plain piece of paper, folded in thirds.

"What?" the cop said.

Silent, she handed him the note.

I am the man for you. The others will be elimi-
nated one by one.
Your cop is up next.

"Shit," the officer said, and pulled out his cell phone.

Bella allowed herself a moment of panic, a full sixty seconds, before she grabbed her purse and keys.

"No, no one's come or gone that shouldn't be here," the cop was saying into his phone. When he'd disconnected, he walked Bella to her car, his gaze vigilant and alert. "Where are you going?" he asked her.

She sighed. The only place she'd probably ever intended to end up tonight, in spite of the fact that she had no idea why he wanted her there. And at the moment, none of that mattered. The note had been a clear warning—he was in danger.

Because of her. "Jacob's."

He nodded, and as he watched her drive off, pulled out his cell phone again.

On the road, she pulled out her own cell phone and called Jacob.

"Jesus," he said in clear relief. "I just heard from Ethan, and I've been going nuts."

"I had protection."

"Yes, but I still want you out of the apartment," he said in an unmistakable demand.

"Already ahead of you."

In the following beat of silence she could hear his anger that she'd left her protection behind. "Where are you? I'll call an escort—"

"I'm halfway there. I'm on Highway 1 already."

"Jesus, you must be flying."

"Do you have a squad car there? Are you protected?"

"Yes." His voice softened. "It's going to be okay, Bella."

"The eliminating part," she managed to say. "That's a little troublesome."

"We'll protect them."

"You," she said, throat tight. "I'm worried about *you*, Jacob. And here I am, on my way to your house, maybe leading someone right to you." Oh, God.

She looked in her rearview mirror. Light traffic. No way to tell if anyone was following her. "I can't do this. I'm not coming to you."

"Yes, you are," he said in that same calm, even voice, and only because she knew him did she hear the undertone of anger and worry.

For her. "Jacob—"

"Listen to me. If you don't come here, I'm going to get on my motorcycle to come get you, and I'm on narcotics, Bella. It won't be pretty." He softened his voice. "Please. Please come here. *Now*."

Okay, so the domineering "now" ruined the "please" but she nodded. She would do as he asked, and once again she'd be with him, spend time with him—not because he *wanted* her to come and stay, but because his sense of protectiveness insisted on it.

Fifteen minutes later, she pulled up his driveway and parked next to the squad car already parked there. She saw Jacob move away from where he'd been talking to his protection. She got a quick glimpse of faded Levi's low on his hips, the splint and nothing else as she opened her car door.

And then he was right there, pulling her in close against that bare, warm chest. His good arm tightened around her, his warm lips brushing her temple. "You're safe now, Bella. I've got you."

She slid her arms around his waist and felt the reassuring bulk of his gun in the back of his waistband. "It's you I'm worried about."

"I'm safe, too."

Yes. Yes, he was, and she sucked in air for the first time since she'd found the note, rubbing her cheek over a hard pec. Melting into him, she let the rest of the world slip away, leaning forward until her head was tucked under his chin.

She was safe in his arms.

Or at least her body was.

She just wasn't nearly so sure about her heart.

14

ETHAN MET THEM AT Jacob's house, and took the note for evidence. Bella called Willow, to tell her about the latest development, and discovered her boss had gone to Trevor's instead because her mother had been hosting bingo for thirty-five seniors. Trevor got on the phone and told Bella to come, as well, but she said she was fine where she was for the night.

And then hoped that was true.

Jacob had left her alone in the living room to give her privacy for her calls, and done with them now, she went to the kitchen. There she grabbed Jacob's pain pills and a glass of water, because she hadn't missed how pale and shaky he'd seemed during the meeting with Ethan, but when she moved down the hall to his bedroom, it was empty.

The bathroom door was open, and the shower was running. She stepped into the steamy room, and thanks to the glass tub enclosure, had a perfect view.

Jacob stood facing the water, his good arm straight out in front of him, braced on the tile, head bent so that the water beat down on his shoulders and back.

"What are you doing?"

He lifted his head. "Cleaning up."

"You'll get your bandage wet."

"It has to be changed anyway."

He reached for the shampoo, and she didn't miss his wince. "Wait." Peeling off her clothes, she stepped into the tub and met his hot, hot gaze.

"That should have been on my fantasy list," he said.

"What?"

"Watching you strip."

"Do you ever think of anything besides me naked?"

He smiled. "I think of me naked, with you."

"Turn and face the water, perv, I'll help you soap up."

When he turned, she wrapped her arms around him from behind, and then, because she couldn't resist, kissed first his good shoulder, and then moved to the other, kissing all around the edge of his bandaging. When she got to the center of his back and pressed her lips to his spine, he sucked in a breath and dropped his head forward with a moan for more.

Pouring some shower gel into her hands, she pressed her body against his so that there wasn't a breath of space between them, and ran her soapy hands over his chest, his abs, and then guiding her fingers downward, wrapped them around his erection.

Another rough groan escaped him and he leaned back into her. "God, Bella."

Her mouth continued to skim over his spine as she stroked the length of him in her slicked-up fingers, apparently applying just the right amount of pressure, because he actually whimpered.

"Okay?" she whispered, sliding her other hand down the front of a rock-hard thigh, then up again to cup him, gently squeezing.

"Christ." His voice was thick and husky. "If I was any more okay, I'd be a puddle on the tile at your feet." He covered her hand with his and stroked himself along with her, showing her how hard he liked it. After a minute, he groaned and pulled away. "Stop," he gasped. "I'm going to come if you keep that up."

She peered around his arm to take in the sight of him fully aroused, wet and glistening, and her mouth actually watered. "Sit."

"What?"

She pushed him down to the tub ledge along the back, then straddled his legs and kissed him.

Gripping her hip with his good hand, he dived into the kiss, taking her mouth roughly, stroking her tongue with his while his one hand ran feverishly over her, gliding over her breasts, cupping and squeezing her ass. "You feel so good," he murmured against her wet skin. Dipping his head, he pulled a nipple into his mouth at the same time his thumb stroked between her thighs, directly over ground zero, and that was it for her.

In that moment, she didn't care what this was, or why she was trying to hold back.

She needed him.

"Inside me," she gasped.

"But you're not ready—"

"I was ready before I even got here." Lifting up, she slid herself down onto his hard, throbbing length all in one motion, fully seating him deep within her.

"Oh, Christ, Bella."

Her body clenched hard, making him groan again.

"Condom," he groaned.

"It's the wrong time of the month." Then she gave him the line he'd so often given her. "It should be okay." She listened to the sound of his quickened breathing, loving how his arm tightened on her as he kissed her throat, a breast, licking his tongue over her nipple as he thrust up within her.

Her arms tightened on him, too, and she shifted restlessly, feeling filled, feeling desperate, feeling so hungry and achy, *needing* him—

Needing.

God, she was half out of her mind with the need, and also halfway to heaven, and only partially aware that she was spreading hot, desperate kisses over his neck in tune to the hot, desperate words she was whispering, "Don't stop, Jacob. Please, don't stop loving me…"

"I won't," he swore, wrapping his good arm solidly around her back as he began to move, flexing his hips, doing his best to meet her thrust for thrust as he kissed, bit and sucked the skin of her neck and throat, all of it turning her on all the more, as if she needed to be any more turned on.

"God, Bella." He paused to devour her mouth again, his tongue tangling with hers. "You're so wet, so tight." He was looking into her eyes, holding her gaze prisoner, and she couldn't look away, didn't want to.

"Mine," she thought he whispered, but then she burst and could hear nothing but the blood rushing through her head and the faint guttural sound of Jacob's rough groan as he came, his entire body contracting with hers, taking her over the edge yet again in a longer, protracted orgasm she wasn't sure she'd survive. Then his mouth touched hers, sharing air, sharing everything he had, and there were no more thoughts.

FOR A WEEK NOTHING MORE happened on the case. No shootings, no notes, nothing out of the ordinary. The men on Bella's date list were still watched and protected to the best of the P.D.'s ability, but every day that passed seemed to drain some of the urgency away.

Not Jacob. He remained frustrated and worried

about Bella's safety, especially given that his shooting arm was, well, shot.

But he was glad for the reprieve from more death and mayhem. It gave him time to obsess over whatever he'd done to make Bella pull back.

Not physically.

Physically, they were still setting records for condom usage and the number of times they could drive each other insane in bed.

And out of it.

But emotionally…emotionally Bella had changed, albeit so slightly it was hard to be sure. Still, ever since that day after his shooting, when Austin had walked in on them, she hadn't been quite as open, quite as…his.

And nothing he did seemed to bring her back. The only time she allowed any kind of connection with him was when they were making love. And that should have been enough.

But it wasn't.

Another adjustment was the whole being off work. For the first time in years, he wasn't working 24/7, and he…liked it.

He liked it a lot.

He liked having free time, which he did his best to spend with Bella. She and Willow were determined to reclaim Edible Bliss and get over the shootings, and their customer base was slowly returning, but when she wasn't toiling away in the kitchen, she came out to be with him.

He'd played the injured-patient card for the first few days, and had indeed coaxed a Nurse Bella out of the deal. And then, though he was up and about, he managed to still need her help with as many tasks that involved dressing and undressing as possible.

She'd been game.

So maybe he'd imagined the other, the slight pulling back. Maybe it was just her way of keeping it "casual" like they'd agreed.

If so, he had to respect that.

And so it was that one week after getting shot, he'd conned Austin into bringing Shenanigans takeout for him and Bella. She was due off work any time, and had said she'd drive over.

He'd have preferred to take her out in person. Maybe for paddle boarding, or kayaking. Or a ride on his bike.

Something wild and fun and adventurous.

But he was still so limited. The shoulder was healing, but slowly, *painfully* slowly. He'd started physical therapy, except it would be a month yet before he had full movement.

At least his doctor had promised to clear him back to desk duty next week.

Woo hoo. Desk duty. He could hardly wait.

Austin let himself in and set down the bag in the kitchen. "Where's the wife?"

"Funny."

"No, what's funny is that you think I'm kidding."

Jacob pulled out the containers of food and...a couple of X-rated magazines. He slid a look at Austin.

"What? You're married, not dead."

"Will you stop with the married thing? We're just...seeing each other."

Austin snorted.

"What?"

"Jacob, she has a drawer of her stuff in your bathroom."

"So?"

"So when a woman has a drawer in a guy's house, it's *not* casual."

"It's just while I'm recuperating."

"Really? So when you're back to work, you're going to tell her the license for the drawer is revoked?"

Jacob opened his mouth, and then shut it.

Shit.

He hadn't thought of it like that. Hell, he'd not thought of it at all.

"Look," Austin said, taking pity on him. "As a cop, you're careful, methodical. It's what makes you so great at the work. But you suck at the real-life shit."

"I do not."

"Real-life shit can't be run off a careful, methodical plan of attack, man. Or by the book. Sometimes you have to wing it. Sometimes you have to go with the flow."

"I can go with the flow as good as the next guy."

Austin wasn't buying it. "Going with the flow would mean accepting that Bella isn't just a casual fling. That things have changed, and you want more with her."

"More doesn't work out for me, remember?"

"Yeah, but that was when you were with the wrong women, and when you were just a badass detective and nothing else."

"What are you talking about? I'm still a detective."

Austin eyed Jacob's board shorts, which was all he was wearing. "No, now you're also part beach bum apparently. Maybe *that* guy could go for more and keep it."

"Would you quit it already. We're just messing around." There wasn't more, there couldn't be, even if he sometimes lately found himself wishing for it. No woman in her right mind would want more from a cop, and he knew this from personal experience.

"Hey, guys."

They both whipped around to find Bella in the doorway.

"Didn't mean to startle you," she said. "I knocked, but no one answered."

As usual, she was a sight for sore eyes. She wore a knit top that crisscrossed her breasts and was the color of her eyes, with a short denim skirt that made the best of her mouthwatering legs. Jacob headed for her, pulling her in, pressing his mouth to her jaw, then her lips, and though she met his kiss, it seemed devoid of its usual wattage. "You okay?" he asked, running his good hand down her arm.

"Always."

"You kids enjoy," Austin said, and pulled Jacob away from Bella in the guise of giving him a brotherly noogie. "You might want to explain that 'just messing around' comment to her," he whispered.

But Jacob knew that no explanation was necessary, not for Bella, who'd set the rules herself. He shoved Austin out the door and smiled at Bella. "Hungry?"

Her gaze met his, a little too shuttered for his liking, but she was smiling warmly and was clearly happy to see him. "Starving," she murmured.

WHEN BELLA OPENED HER EYES a few hours later, it was ten o'clock at night and the sun was long gone. Jacob was asleep beside her, both of them naked. They were sideways in his bed, blankets and sheets long ago tossed to the floor.

Jacob was on his back, his good arm being used as her pillow. She'd thrown a leg over him and had drooled on his chest. Carefully she untangled herself, rolled off the bed and began to search out the various articles of clothing that had been strewn around the room.

Jacob had been right. He was recovering nicely, and had proven it.

Three times.

She slipped into her clothes, grabbed her sandals, and tiptoed to the bedroom door.

"Hey."

With a grimace, she plastered on a smile and only when she was sure it was light and casual—God, how she'd grown to hate that word—did she turn. "Hey."

Sprawled out, lit only by the moonlight slanting in his window, Jacob sent her a lazy smile, a wicked smile, the kind that suggested maybe a late-night snack to regain some strength, and then another heart-stopping round of naked fun. "Where're you going?"

She hesitated. "I thought I'd stay at Willow's mom's tonight."

"Bella, it's late. I don't want you driving back into town now."

Then ask me to stay...

"Stay," he said.

Oh, God. Her heart actually skipped a beat as hope and affection and something far trickier all tangled for space in her heart, which had just lodged itself in her throat. She held her breath and moved closer to the bed. "Why?" she whispered.

"I just said why, it's late."

Disappointment nearly choked her. No worries. She'd go home and drown it out with chocolate. "I have to get up early anyway, and you don't. You need your rest."

He sat up, the muscles in his abs crunching.

God, he was beautiful. It wasn't fair just how beautiful, and with a sigh, she leaned in to kiss him.

She couldn't help herself.

He cupped the back of her head and deepened the kiss, fisting his hand in her hair, pressing her in toward him until she began to melt.

She knew what would come next.

Her clothes would fall away again and then he'd put that mouth on her, that talented, greedy, knowing mouth, and she'd never leave.

She'd never want to.

Which was why she was going, dammit. Sleeping with him was doing something to her, making her want things she had no business wanting, not from him. Knowing it, she forced herself to pull away, forced her hands into her pockets and her eyes off his. "If you keep that up," she quipped, "I'll never go."

"Maybe you've discovered my evil plan," he murmured, his naked body calling to hers.

Maybe, he'd said.

Did that mean he wasn't certain? She wasn't sure, but it sounded to her like he wasn't ready to admit that he wanted her to stay. Not because he needed help, not because she was in danger, but because he wanted *her.*

That settled her mind as nothing else could have.

Dammit.

It was her hang-up, not his, but she couldn't ignore

it. Not when her flight reflex was suddenly screaming. At the door, she turned back to look at him, and found his dark eyes on hers, silent and assessing. Her throat tightened, her eyes burned. "I'll see you later," she said, and left before he could touch her again with his magic body and change her mind.

15

THEY DID A WASH AND repeat for three days, with Bella coming over to Jacob's after work, and then leaving late at night.

There'd been no more shootings and though Edible Bliss hadn't reopened to the public, they were still operating the kitchen for their direct-to-restaurant customers. Willow was back in her apartment, being watched over by the cops, but she'd asked Bella to be around whenever possible.

Which is how Jacob once again found himself lying on his bed, watching Bella gather her things to leave. Two minutes ago he'd come so hard he'd been rendered blind, deaf and dumb.

Hell, he still couldn't feel his legs. Somebody had taken out all his bones.

Not Bella. She'd put herself back together with alarming ease.

Jacob didn't move or change his breathing because

if he did, he'd sit up and ask—beg—to know why she had to go.

Why she seemed to want his body plenty, but didn't want to sleep with him.

At first, he'd shrugged it off. They'd said casual, and she'd certainly kept it that. Besides, how could he complain? He was getting fantastic, mind-blowing sex without the worry or awkwardness of the morning after.

And given their typical humiliating morning after—what he referred to as the Raspberry Incident came to mind—he should be fine with that.

Which in no way explained why it was bugging the hell out of him. Maybe because it meant he was far more vested in this than she, and he hated that. She was happy enough to see him, hang out with him, he knew this. In fact, she seemed more than happy.

She glowed.

But just how content could she really be if she couldn't wait to leave him at the end of the evening in spite of the looming, omnipresent danger?

There had to be a reason. He just didn't know what. He was missing something, something big. But for two nights in a row, he'd let her go without a word because it was embarrassing that he wanted more than she did, and also because he didn't want the inevitable confrontation that might facilitate their end.

The end of the happiest he'd been in too damn long.

But he couldn't do it any longer, couldn't keep quiet. "Why do you always go?"

She went still for a beat, then turned back from the door. "What?"

"You heard me."

"It's late, Jacob."

"But that's the very reason you should stay."

She was quiet a moment, just looking at him, and he knew right then—he'd most definitely missed something, but hell if he could figure out what. "I'll come with you."

"Not necessary," she said. "I have to get up really early."

It was his turn to be quiet a minute. "Are you afraid to let me go to your place because we haven't caught the shooter?"

"Partly."

"Then stay here."

"Another reason I leave is because I don't live here," she said. "Actually, I don't really live anywhere."

"What does that mean?"

She turned back to the door, which frustrated the hell out of him because now he couldn't see her face. "It means maybe I've been thinking it's time to move on again."

"You've been thinking about moving on?" Listen to that, listen to him sounding all cool and calm, when he suddenly felt anything but. "Since when?"

"I always think about it."

He pushed off the bed and moved toward her,

taking her purse out of her hands, backing her to the wall. "Where will you go this time?"

"Don't know yet."

"Why now?"

"Why not? There's really no reason to stay...."

He cupped her face with one hand and made her look at him. "No reason?"

"It's not like I have my own shop, or a real relationship. I mean, we're just messing around..."

Jesus. He stared at her, his thoughtless words to Austin coming back to haunt him. *Hello, missing piece to the puzzle.* "You know what I meant by that, right?"

"Yes," she said. "I believe it's fully self-explanatory."

He shook his head as unaccustomed desperation welled up from within him. Not knowing what to do with it, he pressed her against the wall and kissed her. He kissed her until she softened and slid her hands up his chest, around his neck and clung.

He'd never been one to crave physical closeness, but having Bella in his arms suited him.

It suited him a lot.

Only, Bella had changed the rules, the game, *everything,* turning it all upside and sideways on him.

And she was leaving.

Right now, unless he said something to fix it, to bridge the big, gaping hole between them. He opened his mouth and let out the first thing that came to him. "Santa Rey has a lot to offer you. Your pastries are already gaining fame, and Willow told me she suggested you create a Web site. You could go huge, Bella. Right here."

"I don't think this is about my job," she said.

"Is this about *my* job?"

She just looked at him.

Quick, Madden, think quick. "I've never been with a woman who could handle my work."

"A woman who chooses to be in your life should accept you, Jacob, just as you are."

"Should. But they don't. Look at you, running for the door."

"My leaving has nothing to do with your job. Or changing anything about you." She cocked her head and studied him. "Would you ask me to change?"

Would he? Would he get down on bended knee and beg her not to leave here when the time came, simply because he needed her?

"Because I'd never ask you to change who and what you are, Jacob. Never." With that, she went up on her tiptoes and pressed her mouth to his temple. "'Night."

"Bella—"

"It's late," she murmured, pressing her lips to his other temple, his jaw, and then far too briefly, his lips. "Gotta get some sleep. You're starting work tomorrow, you should get some sleep, too."

And then she was gone.

TWO DAYS LATER, BELLA and Willow were just closing up the kitchen when Jacob came in the back door with two cops, one on either side of him. He thanked them and they went back to their perch outside.

One look at Jacob had Bella's heart taking a good, hard leap. She could tell herself that she was good and fine and well with everything that had happened until she was blue in the face.

But she was one big, fancy liar.

She wasn't good and fine, not when every muscle in her body tensed with the urge to run across the kitchen and throw herself at him.

He'd gone back to work, and for two days had been buried under by the backlog, hardly coming up for air. Or so he claimed when he called her at night.

As for her, she'd been…well, she'd been thinking entirely too much.

But no matter how much she'd been remembering and reliving, the reality of Jacob in the flesh was so much more potent than the memories.

He wore a dark suit and tie and his splint, and he looked disturbingly…hot.

"Wow," Willow murmured, leaning back against the sink, looking him over with heated eyes. "You clean up nice, Detective."

"Thanks." He didn't take his gaze off Bella. And those eyes were filled with frustration, temper, hunger and so much bafflement that Bella didn't know whether to laugh or get rid of Willow so she could have him right here in the kitchen.

"You hungry?" she asked.

"Yes."

Not for food.

Those words went unspoken, but they shimmered in the air between them.

Willow had a bag of popcorn, her favorite lunch, and was dividing a curious stare between them as if they were the latest number-one movie at the box office.

Finally, Bella looked at her, brow raised.

"Oh!" Willow let out a little laugh and grabbed her purse. "I'm out." She looked back at them. "Don't do anything I wouldn't do and just so you know, that doesn't cover a lot of ground."

Jacob smiled at her, then turned his attention back to Bella, not saying a word, just giving her that look that never failed to make her nipples hard and her panties wet. "So," she murmured. "A suit?"

"I was due in court this morning, had to testify on a case."

"Did it go well?"

"Yes." His eyes never left her face as he reached out and slowly pulled her in. "Missed you, Bella."

Her heart took another hard leap against her ribs. At this rate, she'd be in heart-attack territory in under five minutes. "You did?"

He pressed his forehead to hers. "Yeah. I'm hot and starving. Come with me, let's get a pizza and go to my house. It's going to be a full moon. We can take the horses out on a moonlight ride."

"The moon doesn't come up until late."

He slid her a long look that said *this again?* "So stay, instead of driving back."

Her throat tightened. No. No, dammit. She wasn't going to go through this again. She couldn't. Not when she knew she was hopelessly, pathetically falling for him. "I can't." It took her another extremely long minute—where she pressed her nose into his throat and just inhaled him as if maybe it was going to be the very last time—before she forced herself to pull free. "I can't tonight."

"But—"

"I can't," she repeated. "Listen, I have to go. Let yourself out." And grabbing a wet cloth, left him to go wipe down the tables in the front room, even though they were perfectly clean since they still didn't have walk-in customers.

She ended up just standing there, staring sightlessly at nothing.

When, finally, she heard the back door close, she sagged into a chair and covered her face.

The front door opened and Trevor popped his head in. He was wearing surf shorts and a weather-guard tee, and his usual contagious smile. "Hey, what are you doing? I'm going sailing. Come with, it's gorgeous outside—" He broke off, looking her over. "You okay?"

"Yes."

"Liar." He took the towel out of her hands,

crouched at her side and cupped her face. "You know what you need?"

"A one-way ticket to the South Pacific?"

"A sail," he said gently. "With no worries, no plans, nothing but a few waves. Come on, baby, let me show you a good time."

It was such a cheesy line that she managed to laugh, as he'd intended, and he smiled into her face. "Attagirl."

JACOB WENT HOME AND stared at his empty house. He looked at his living room and pictured Bella standing before the huge windows, eyeing the view. He saw her sitting on the couch with that light of wicked intent in her eyes. He saw her sitting on his kitchen counter.

He couldn't even look at his bed.

Or his shower...

Her presence was here in every room of his house, and in every part of his heart.

He was such an idiot. He wasn't just messing around with her. Why hadn't he told her that?

He could say this was casual until he was blue in the face, he could pretend with the best of them that he was okay with her walking away from Santa Rey, away from him, but he wasn't okay with it and he never would be.

And he owed it to her to at least have the balls to say so.

Undoubtedly, he'd get his stupid heart broken for the effort, but hell if he'd let her go without at least putting it all out there on the line. That decided, he whipped out his cell phone and called her. It went right to voice mail, and he absently rubbed his aching shoulder as he left her a message. "Call me, Bella. I'm coming back to the shop, I need to see you, we need to talk." He paused, wondering if he'd sounded too scary and would maybe cause her to bolt before he could get there. "I told you that I miss you," he said, drawing a deep breath. "But what I should have also said was that I love you." Hoping that would cover everything, he started to close his phone, then added, "I'm on my way. Please—" He closed his eyes. "Please be there."

BELLA'S PHONE WAS ON SPEAKER, so both she and Trevor heard the message.

"Sweet," Trevor said. "A little too little too late, but very sweet."

She was driving, but she took a quick look over at him. How had she never seen the menace just beneath his surface before? And now that she had, how the hell was she going to get out of this without getting hurt? Or worse. "If I don't call him back, he's going to come over."

"Yes. And find you already gone." He affected a regretful expression. "So sad."

"He'll look for me."

"No, he won't. He'll see that your duffel bag is gone—thanks for staying packed, by the way, I've got your bag in my trunk. Face it, Jacob is going to assume you've done what you've been talking about, that you've left town. Which you are doing. He won't try to come after you. He has far too much pride and testosterone for that."

She'd have thought so, too, until that phone call. In his voice had been bare, heart-wrenching emotion.

For her.

"Turn right at the marina, Bella."

She didn't want to.

She wanted to turn left and get back on the freeway and head north to Jacob's house. She wanted to reverse time, to the time before she'd told Jacob to let himself out, the implication being that he should let himself out of her life while he was at it.

She wanted to plant both her feet in the ground and make roots. She wanted to tell him she loved him, too, so very much.

Why hadn't she told him?

"Turn right," Trevor repeated softly, and gestured with the gun he had pointed at her.

She turned right.

16

WHEN JACOB GOT BACK to the shop, it was empty. He went upstairs and knocked on Bella's door.

Across the narrow hallway, Willow's door opened and she poked her head out. With tears in her eyes, she shook her head. "She's gone."

"What?"

Willow handed him a note. "This was taped to my door."

Thanks, Willow, for the lovely memories. I'll never forget you, but it's time to move on.

Willow sniffed. "Lord, I'm going to miss that girl."

Jacob's heart had pretty much stopped at the "she's gone" but he read the note again, looking at the hand-writing. Neat, and legible.

His heart started again, with a dull thudding that echoed in his ears.

"What is it?" Willow asked.

"It isn't Bella's writing." Or if it was, she was trying to tell them something. He ran down the stairs and found Tom in the lot. "Did you see Bella leave?"

"No," Tom said. "I just got here. Hang on, I'll check with Scott, who I relieved." He pulled out his cell.

So did Jacob, and immediately called Ethan. "We have a problem."

"That's okay, being as I'm the solution king today," Ethan said. "Did you know that the marina started fingerprinting people to store their boats? The chief told me just today. He found out when he went to store his new boat. It's a new security system, letting people in the gate by their prints."

"Fascinating, but—"

"So the chief puts his fingerprint in, and starts to think. The first shooting, we found that tread, with the marina sand. We canvassed the docks, all the hotels and motels on the marina, ran the boat owners, and found no one connected to Bella. But the fingerprint list doesn't just include the owners, but anyone they allow to use their boat. I'm only halfway through the log and I've already found two of the Edible Bliss's regular customers, the coffee shop guy who was Bella's fourth date, and her coworker, Trevor Mann."

"Trevor," Jacob repeated slowly, just as Tom hung up his phone.

"Yeah, his stepfather owns a thirty-two-foot Morgan," Ethan said.

"Trevor and Bella left twenty-five minutes ago out the front," Tom reported. "We were watching for unauthorized people going out only—"

"Tom says Bella left with Trevor," Jacob told Ethan. "And there's a note here from her saying she's leaving town."

"On Trevor's sailboat?"

"Doesn't say, but I can tell you if the note was written by Bella, it was written under duress."

There was a beat of silence. "You sure?"

"I'd bet my life on it," Jacob said.

"Okay, so she's a missing person."

"Yeah. I'll meet you at the marina."

BELLA WATCHED AS THE MARINA came into view, and her stomach cramped. This wasn't going to be good. "I still don't get why you're doing this."

"Don't you?" Trevor asked.

"No!"

"You were meant for me, Bella."

She stared at him. He looked so normal. How could someone who looked so normal be so insane?

"Breathe, Bella," he reminded her gently.

"Look, if we go back now, I'll talk to the police for you. I'll help explain that you need help, and that—"

"I don't need help. I got what I wanted, and that's

you." He stroked a finger down her jaw and she shuddered.

"Don't worry," he said very softly. "It's going to be okay."

She sincerely doubted that. She really wished she'd finished those self-defense classes. If she had, she'd probably have been able to come up with a better escape plan then having an overdue panic attack.

"Turn here into the parking lot," Trevor told her.

She wondered if she could slow down enough to jump right out of the car. Maybe. But an older man was walking along the sidewalk. What if she jumped out of the car and it ran him over?

"Ten points for the old guy," Trevor said lightly, a small smile in place.

"You're sick."

"Aw. I'm just a guy in love."

"I'm sorry." She shook her head. "This just doesn't make sense. If you wanted me so badly, why didn't you ask me out?"

"I did."

"No, you joked about it, I never thought you were serious."

"Your mistake."

No kidding! "Why did you stop the shooting spree? You only hit three out of eight."

"I shot Seth because you liked him. A lot."

Oh, God, Bella thought, sorrow nearly choking her.

"I shot B.J. because he kept calling you and asking

you out. I tried to shoot Tyler just because he was bugging the shit out of me with all that snooty talk. How could you stand him?"

When she didn't answer, he went on, unperturbed. "None of the others posed a threat until Jacob. God-damn perfect Jacob."

Bella took her eyes off the road to stare at him with a mirthless laugh. "He only started coming around because you started shooting people! How did you get the information on my eight dates?"

He shrugged. "I know one of the coordinators, and he let me get on his computer to let me do some research. I neglected to tell him the research was you. And later, Jacob."

"Oh, my God. If you would have stayed *sane,* I'd never have seen him again."

"Yeah." Trevor let out a long-suffering sigh. "Maybe I made a mistake there. But it wasn't nec-essarily *his* feelings for *you* that got him shot." He paused. "It was your feelings for him. With Jacob around, screwing you senseless, you didn't give me the time of day." He looked at her solemnly. "You'll have to forget him now, Bella. He might be the big, strong, silent type, but there's a limit to a guy like that. He'll never be romantic and sweet and loving. I'll be that guy for you, I swear it."

"No, you won't," she told him. "I love him. I love him for exactly who he is. You can kidnap me and force me to be with you—" Only until she got a chance to run like hell. "But I will not stop loving him."

"Yes, you will."

Resisting the urge to thunk her head into the steering wheel and put herself out of her misery, she pulled into the parking lot, brain racing for a plan. Maybe she could keep him talking until…until what? No one was going to save her. She'd been seen leaving with Trevor, who no one had ever considered a threat.

But maybe…maybe if Jacob went back for her like he said and saw the note that Trevor had made her write, maybe he'd realize that she was trying to leave him a clue…

"We're going to go sailing on a nice, long vacation," Trevor said. "And live the way you've always lived, taking each day at a time. It's how you love to do things, right? No ties, no hold to anyone or any place."

That was true, that's how she'd always lived. But that no longer made her happy—not that she planned on sharing that life-altering epiphany with Trevor. "You can't make me stay with you."

"We'll be out on the open sea, you won't have a choice. If we stay out long enough, you'll fall in love with me the way I love you."

The way he loved her was koo-koo crazy, but she kept her mouth shut.

"Park here," he said, pointing to a spot. "Out of the car."

She got out of the car, and extremely aware of the gun, she kept silent.

For now.

Trevor stepped out, as well, his eyes on her. His hand was in his pocket.

On the gun. "Slowly, Bella," he said. "We're going to walk to the building. No funny stuff, we don't want anyone to get hurt."

She bit back a sharp laugh that probably would have sounded hysterical anyway and tried to appeal to reason, assuming he had any left in his addled brain. "Trevor, this is ridiculous. Jacob isn't going to believe I just up and left without a goodbye."

"He'll move on to another woman easily enough. He wasn't looking for anything permanent, remember? You were just a quickie, a one-night stand that extended a few extra nights, that's all."

Only yesterday she might have been willing to believe that, but she'd seen the look in Jacob's eyes this morning. She'd heard it in his voice, and when it counted, he'd given her the words.

He loved her.

"I'm never going to love you, Trevor. I'm going to escape at the first opportunity and you're going to go to jail for murder and attempted murder two times over, not to mention kidnapping."

His jaw tightened. "You need to be quiet now."

"*Murder*, Trevor," she repeated. "You're going to sit in jail and—"

"Christ, I said shut up!" He accompanied this by putting the gun right in her face.

She gulped and closed her mouth, hoping that *someone* would notice the insane guy with the gun, but naturally there wasn't another soul anywhere to be seen.

Trevor shoved his gun back in his pocket and took Bella's hand. "Better. Now we're going to walk into the marina, smile, then get on my boat and sail away. You're going to behave."

"I don't tend to 'behave.'" Well, actually, there'd been that one night, when Jacob had handcuffed her to the bed and they'd spent some fun role-playing bad cop/bad girl, but she was pretty sure that wasn't what Trevor meant.

Surely there would be someone inside that she could recruit to help her...

They walked into the marina building, hand in hand like lovers. The large reception area on the right was filled with open seating facing huge wall-to-wall windows that revealed the docks and the ocean beyond. Another wall was lined with vending machines, and a third was wallpapered with a map of the planet.

The place was empty except for a teenage girl sitting behind the reception desk. She was reading Cosmo and texting at the same time, her thumbs a whirl of motion.

Bella looked at her and felt the first wave of despair. She couldn't involve this girl and risk Trevor getting trigger happy with her, not when he'd proven how easily he could kill.

So Bella said nothing as Trevor pulled her over to the far double glass doors. There, he pressed his thumb to a small screen, and the doors clicked open. "New security," he said proudly, and pulled her through. "You have to be a boat owner or on file as a guest to get to the docks."

Bella dragged her feet along the dock. All she knew was that she didn't want to get on the sailboat. If she did, and Trevor was able to get them out to sea, she was in big trouble. Maybe she could fall into the water, or just start screaming. Or—

"Don't," Trevor said in her ear, his hand gripping hers hard.

"I didn't do anything."

"You're thinking it."

She was. She was also thinking if she shoved him hard enough, he might fall in, and—

"I'll shoot you on my way down."

Yeah. Yeah, he probably would. Note to self: next time try to wade the psychos out of your friendship pool. "How do you possibly imagine you're going to be able to keep me on the boat?"

His eyes gleamed. "I have my ways."

Oh, good. He had his ways. Lucky her.

"Don't forget, Bella. You *will* behave."

Uh-huh. She'd get right on that.

His Morgan sailboat was in the sixth of eight slots, with the last two being empty. No help there. It was blue and white with teakwood trim, and looked well loved and cared for.

"Home sweet home," Trevor said.

She eyed the door that led to belowdecks, where there was undoubtedly a place he planned on restraining her. Her stomach cramped at the thought.

Now or never, Bella...

"Get on," Trevor said.

Stall. Run. Make a scene! "I'm hungry," she said, albeit a little wildly. "We should go back and get some food—"

"Get on *now*."

"But we need—"

"I have everything you'll ever need, Bella. Trust me."

Like hell. "I need sunscreen—50 SPF. I bet you didn't get 50 SPF—"

"Get. On."

He added a little shove to this command and it was either fall into the water or board.

She took a big gulp of air, hoped a bullet couldn't travel through water—probably if she'd paid better attention in high school physics class she might know this—and jumped off the dock.

JACOB MADE IT TO THE marina in five minutes by running just about every red light and hitting Highway 1 at seventy-five miles per hour.

When he pulled into the parking lot, Ethan was

just getting out of his car, and they met up with a handful of others led by Ramon Castillo.

"Trevor Mann's boat is in slip D06," Ethan told them, consulting his pad.

The marina was large, and had five rows of docking that stretched into the bay like fingers. There were hundreds of boats, but not nearly as many people—the place looked completely deserted.

As they stormed their way into the building toward the docks, a shot rang out in the air, echoing over the water.

17

THE MOMENT BELLA plunged into the water, she heard the shot ring out, and involuntarily screamed.

Not a good idea underwater.

She inhaled a cold lungful and promptly choked, forcing her back to the surface. She gasped quickly and plunged beneath again, bumping hard into the hull of the boat and knocking the air right out of herself. *Good going, Bella. You get away from the crazy stalker and then try to help him kill you.*

Still beneath the water, she struggled with the strong urge to kick to the surface again, and just before she had to have air, someone splashed into the water next to her. Propelled by the momentum, again she hit the hull, hard. She didn't scream this time, she didn't have the air left. And she had even less when two hands grabbed her.

Trevor.

Oh, no. Hell, no. In that moment, her fear was

replaced by fury. Because of Trevor, Jacob would think she'd run away, think she was yet another woman who didn't believe he was worth fighting for. Because of Trevor, Willow would accept her skipping out as just part of her pattern. Because of Trevor, her chance to change had been taken away from her.

So she fought back. Reaching up, she closed her hands around his throat, squeezing as hard as she could, which wasn't hard enough.

She was too weak, and this wasn't going to work. Frustrated, she shoved him, trying to swim away down the narrow space between the slip and the boat.

She heard a dull thud. Trevor's hands fell from her neck, but before she could assimilate that, two more hands grabbed her and hauled her up to the surface.

She came up swinging, and managed to get in a good punch to the gut.

"Shit!" said someone who definitely wasn't Trevor.

Yet another set of arms slipped around her. "I've got her."

This voice she knew, and immediately she relaxed into the hard wall of muscle. *"Jacob."*

He hauled her in close, holding her above water. "I've got you, Bella. You're safe."

She always was safe with him, she thought, blinking water out of her eyes as he lifted her up to someone on the dock already reaching for her.

Ethan.

He set her down but her knees were weak and she dropped to them. Directly in front of them was Trevor, facedown and being cuffed by a handful of uniformed men. He had blood flowing from a gash on the back of his head.

"You knocked him off me." She coughed as Jacob was pulling up out of the water.

"No." He dropped to his knees in front of her, running his hands over her as if he needed to make sure for himself that she was okay. "That was all you. You smashed his head against the concrete pillar under the dock. Nice going, by the way."

She stared at the boat that Trevor had planned to force her onto, the water she'd been pulled out of and then into Jacob's eyes.

"You did amazing," he said softly, taking a blanket from a uniformed officer and tugging it around her shoulders. "You were in a bad situation and you kept your head. I'm so proud of you, Bella."

The words bathed her in desperately needed warmth. Weak and shaking from the adrenaline letdown, she dropped her head to his shoulder. She'd barely dragged in a breath before he wrapped his arms around her hard and shuddered. "I thought I'd lost you. I don't want to ever lose you."

"I wasn't leaving. Not willingly anyway." She lifted her head, needing to see his face. "I didn't want to leave you, Jacob. I know I was sending mixed signals, but that's because I didn't want to push you into this. I thought you weren't ready, that you needed more time."

He shook his head. "I don't need more time. I love you, Bella."

"I love you, too," she whispered. She hadn't gotten the words out before he lowered his head and kissed her.

An EMT dropped beside them with his med kit. "She needs to be checked out, looks like she hit her head, too."

Yeah. Now that he mentioned it, she was feeling a little dizzy...

Jacob looked deep into her eyes, his clouded with worry. "Stay with me," he said, repeating her words from when he'd been shot back to her.

"I'm okay," she promised. "I'm not going to faint."

His laugh was nothing more than a breath against her temple. "I meant here. With me. Stay here with me. Because I want you with me more than anything else."

"You mean, here in Santa Rey?"

"In Australia. In goddamn Timbuktu. I don't care where, as long as we're in the same place."

The warmth from the blanket and his own body continued to seep into her, but the warmth from his words penetrated even deeper, heating her from the inside out. "Yes, I'll stay," she breathed. "For as long as you want me."

His smile spread across his face. "That's going to be a while. Forever a while."

"I can't think of anything I could want more."

* * * * *

COMING NEXT MONTH

Available August 31, 2010

HBCNM0810

HARLEQUIN®

A Romance

FOR EVERY MOOD™

Spotlight on
Heart & Home

Heartwarming romances
where love can happen
right when you least expect it.

See the next page to enjoy a sneak peek
from Harlequin Superromance®,
a Heart and Home series.

Enjoy a sneak peek at fan favorite Molly O'Keefe's
Harlequin Superromance miniseries,
THE NOTORIOUS O'NEILLS, *with*
TYLER O'NEILL'S REDEMPTION,
available September 2010
only from Harlequin Superromance.

Police chief Juliette Tremblant recognized the shape of the man strolling down the street—in as calm and leisurely fashion as if it were the middle of the day rather than midnight. She slowed her car, convinced her eyes were playing tricks on her. It had been a long time since Tyler O'Neill had been seen in this town.

As she pulled to a stop at the curb, he turned toward her, and her heart about stopped.

"What the hell are you doing here, Tyler?"

"Well, if it isn't Juliette Tremblant." He made his way over to her, then leaned down so he could look her in the eye. He was close enough to touch.

Juliette was not, repeat, *not* going to touch Tyler O'Neill. Not with her fingers. Not with a ten-foot pole. There would be no touching. Which was too bad, since it was the only way she was ever going to convince herself the man standing in front of her—as rumpled and heart-stoppingly handsome now as he'd been at sixteen—was real.

And not a figment of all her furious revenge dreams.

"What are you doing back in Bonne Terre?" she asked.

"The manor is sitting empty," Tyler said and shrugged, as though his arriving out of the blue after ten years was casual. "Seems like someone should be watching over the family home."

"You?" She laughed at the very notion of him being here for any unselfish reason. "Please."

He stared at her for a second, then smiled. Her heart fluttered against her chest—a small mechanical bird powered by that smile.

"You're right." But that cryptic comment was all he offered.

Juliette bit her lip against the other questions.

Why did you go?

Why didn't you write? Call?

What did I do?

But what would be the point? Ten years of silence were all the answer she really needed.

She had sworn off feeling anything for this man long ago. Yet one look at him and all the old hurt and rage resurfaced as though they'd been waiting for the chance. That made her mad.

She put the car in gear, determined not to waste another minute thinking about Tyler O'Neill. "Have a good night, Tyler," she said, liking all the cool "go screw yourself" she managed to fit into those words.

It seems Juliette has an old score to settle with Tyler.
Pick up TYLER O'NEILL'S REDEMPTION
to see how he makes it up to her.
Available September 2010,
only from Harlequin Superromance.